THE CORNER HOUSE GIRLS
ON A TOUR

BY

GRACE BROOKS HILL

THE CORNER HOUSE GIRLS ON A TOUR

CHAPTER I—A RED LETTER DAY INDEED

There was a deal of bustle and a twittering like an eager flock of sparrows in the big kitchen of the old Corner House, which stood facing Main Street in Milton, but with its long side and rear yard and garden running far back on Willow Street.

The four Kenway girls had the room all to themselves at this early hour on Saturday morning, for Mrs. MacCall and Aunt Sarah Maltby had not yet come downstairs, while Linda, the maid, had deserted the kitchen and pantry altogether for the time being.

Ruth, the eldest and most sedate of the sisters, was filling sandwiches at the dresser—and such a variety as there was of them!

Chicken, with mayonnaise and a lettuce leaf; pink ham cut thin and decorated with little golden dabs of mustard; peanut butter sandwiches; nut and cheese sandwiches, the filling nestling in a salad leaf, too; tuna fish, with narrow slices of red, red Spanish peppers decorating it; and of course sardines, carefully split and laid between soda crackers. What picnic lunch would be complete without sardines?

Agnes, the next oldest to Ruth and the beauty of the family, was slicing bread as exactly as though it were a problem in geometry and in such quantity that Tess declared it looked as though they were to feed an army.

Tess herself was seriously attending to the boiling of two dozen eggs in a big saucepan.

"Though why you need to watch 'em so closely I can't see," complained Agnes. "There are other things you might be doing when there is so much to do—goodness knows! Those eggs won't get away."

"No," joined in Dot, the youngest of the Corner House girls, and quite seriously, too. "No. It isn't like boiling lobsters."

"Right, Dottums," chuckled Agnes, recovering from her vexation immediately. "Eggs

are an entirely different kind of shellfish."

"Well," said the little girl, explaining, "Mrs. Adams boiled some raw lobsters the other day, and one hopped right out of the pot on to the floor and started for the door—it really did!"

"Oo-ee!" gasped Tess, attracted for a moment from the bobbing eggs by this statement. "The poor thing!"

"Who's a poor thing—Mrs. Adams?" asked Ruth, laughing gayly.

"Why, no," said Tess, who was nothing if not tender-hearted. "The lobster."

"Goodness!" exclaimed Agnes. "Do you s'pose it hurts a lobster to be boiled?"

"Why doesn't it?" demanded Tess, promptly.

"'Cause it has a shell," ventured Dot.

"Why—because they always do boil them," said Agnes, rather at a loss for an answer to Tess' question.

"Sometimes they broil them," said the oldest sister, smiling.

"Well, they're used to it, anyway," declared Agnes, with conviction.

"I—I don't believe anybody could get used to being boiled," observed Tess, slowly. "Look at Sammy Pinkney."

"Where?" demanded Agnes, jumping. "I hope that horrid child isn't coming over so early. I hoped we'd get away without having him around."

"Oh, my!" murmured Dot. "You know he's just got over the scarlet fever."

"But he hasn't got over being a nuisance," declared the older girl.

"I didn't mean that Sammy was really here—to look at," explained the serious Tess. "I meant—I meant——"

"Well, what did you mean?" asked Agnes, who was inclined to be impatient.

"She meant, 'consider Sammy,' didn't you, Tessie?" suggested Ruth, kindly.

"Why—yes."

"Oh! Were you taking him for an example?" cried Agnes. "But Sammy hasn't ever been boiled—although maybe he ought to have been."

"No; he hasn't been boiled," said the serious Tess, still watching the eggs bobbing in the boiling water. "But he's punished lots of times—at school, I mean. And he doesn't seem to get used to it. He hollers just as loud now as the first time I ever heard him."

"Did the lobster holler?" chuckled Agnes. "Did it, Dot?"

But Dot—who was not allowed to "mess in" with the lunch—had found another subject for consideration. She had been looking at Ruth, dexterously opening a second can of sardines. Now, when the cover was laid back and the oil drained off, the smallest girl pointed a dimpled finger at the contents of the can.

"What's the matter, honey?" asked Ruth, smiling down at the serious face of the fairy-like Dot. "What is it?"

"Why, Ruthie," said Dot, wonderingly, "I was only thinking if that middle fish wanted to turn over, what a lot of trouble it would have!"

Amid the laughter of the two older girls at this, the door banged open and a boy with a mop of flaxen hair—a regular "whitehead" and a football cut at that—burst into the room.

"My goodness me, girls! aren't you ready yet?" he demanded. "And it's half-past seven."

"The eggs are," Tess declared, the first to speak, for she had not been laughing.

"Well, then," said the boy, "you and I, Tess, will just take the eggs and go."

"What's the matter, Neale O'Neil? Won't your horse stand?" drawled Agnes, tossing her head.

"We would have been ready long ago if it had not been for you, Neale," said Ruth, promptly.

"How's that? I've been up since five. And the car's right here at the side gate. Cracky! it's a scrumptious auto, girls. I don't believe there ever was a finer."

"When our Mr. Howbridge does anything, he always does it right," proclaimed Tess, giving up the guardianship of the eggs to Ruth. "And Mr. Howbridge had the car built for us."

"But we wouldn't ever have had it," put in Dot, eager to tell all she knew, "if Mrs. Eland and Miss Pepperill hadn't given us the money 'cause we found their Uncle Lemon Aden's money."

"Oh, goodness!" gasped Tess. "Lem-u-el, Dot!"

But Dot ignored the correction. "It was awfully nice of them to give us the car because we found the fortune in our garret."

"Lots you did towards finding it," chuckled Neale O'Neil.

"I'd like to know why I didn't help find it!" cried the smallest Corner House girl, indignantly. "I saw it first—so there! I opened the book it was hid in and I thought it was pitchers."

"Say! that isn't getting us anywhere," began the boy again. "Can't you hurry? Just think! the first ride in your car!"

"Don't remind me," gasped Agnes, cutting a crooked slice. "My nerves are all jumping now like—like a delightful toothache!"

"Glory! listen to her," laughed Neale. "But say, Miss Ruthiford Ten-ways, why do you say that it is my fault that you are not all ready?"

"Because we have to put up lunch enough to satisfy your appetite," said Ruth, running cold water on the eggs from the open faucet.

"Well! I like that!" said Neale.

"I fancy you will, sonny," said Agnes, looking at him slyly. "There are lots of goodies in it."

"Now run and get your hats and wraps, children," commanded Ruth seizing the last two slices of bread Agnes had cut. "That will do, Aggie. Leave a little bread for the folks to eat to-day while we're gone. That basket is all packed, Neale, and you may take it out and put it in the tonneau."

"Oh, my!" gasped Agnes, clasping her hands. "Doesn't that sound fine?"

"What sounds fine!" asked her boy chum, surreptitiously putting the last crumb of a broken sandwich he had found into his mouth.

"The way Ruth said 'tonneau.' So—so Frenchy and automobily!"

"Why, Aggie!" gasped Tess, in amazement, before following Dot out of the kitchen, "you're making up words just like Dot does."

"I feel like making up words," laughed Agnes, who had been "crazy for a car" for months and months! "We'll all be talking about 'tonneaus,' and 'carbureters,' and 'gas,' and 'wiring,' and 'differentials,' and——"

"And 'equilaterals,' and 'isosceles triangles,' and all that," scoffed Neale. "You'll know a hot lot about an automobile, Agamemnon."

"Come, young man!" exclaimed Ruth, tartly, for she was very exact with boys, feeling sure that she did not approve of them—much, "suppose you take the basket out to the car—and these wraps—and this coffee—and the little nursery icebox with the milk bottles—and——"

"Hold on! Hold on!" yelled Neale O'Neil. "What do you think I have—as many arms as a spider? I can't do it all in one trip."

"Well, you might make a beginning," suggested Ruth. "Come, Aggie. Don't moon there all day."

"I'm not," said her next youngest sister. "I'm thinking."

"What's the difference?" demanded Neale, filling his arms with several of the things indicated by Ruth and making for the door.

"I was thinking," said Agnes, quite seriously for her, "what a difference this is from what we were before we came to Milton and the old Corner House to live."

Neale had gone out. Ruth looked at her with softer eyes. Ruth was not exactly pretty, but she had a very sweet face. Everybody said so. Now she looked her understanding at Agnes.

"I know, dear—I know," she said, in her low, full, sweet voice. "This is like another world."

"Or a dream," said Agnes. "Do—do you suppose we'll ever wake up, Ruthie, and find out it's all been make-believe?"

Ruth laughed outright at that and went over and kissed her. "Don't let your imagination run away with you," the older sister said. "It is all real—very real indeed. What could be more real than an automobile—and of our very own?"

Dot came dancing into the room hugging a doll in her arms and cheerfully humming a school song.

"There!" exclaimed Agnes, coming out of the clouds, "I suppose that disreputable Alice-doll has got to go along. It does look awful."

Dot stopped her song at once and her lips pouted.

"She isn't dis—disreput'ble—she isn't!" she cried, stormily. "She's only sick. How would you like it, Aggie Kenway, if you'd been buried alive—andwith dried apples—and had had your complexion spoiled?"

Dot was usually the most peaceful of mortals; but Agnes had touched a sore spot.

"Never mind; you shall take her, love," Ruth said.

"I suppose if we want to go off on a real tour by and by—this coming vacation—Dot'll have to lug that Alice-doll," grumbled Agnes. "Suppose we meet nice people at some of the hotels we stop at, and other little girls have dolls? Dot's will look as though she came from Meadow Street." Meadow Street was in a poor section of Milton.

"I don't care," grumbled Dot; "she's going."

"She ought to go a hospital first," declared Agnes.

"Who ought to go to a hospital?" demanded Neale, coming in again.

"My Alice-doll, Neale," cried Dot, running to him, sure of sympathy—of a kind, at least.

"Well," said the boy, "why not? If folks go to hospitals and get cured, why not dolls?"

"Oh, Neale O'Neil!" gasped Dot, hugging her cherished doll closer.

"Just think how nice Mrs. Eland was to folks in her hospital," went on Neale, his eyes twinkling. "And Doctor Forsyth. A hospital is a mighty fine place."

"But—but what would they do to my Alice-doll?" asked the smallest girl, seriously.

"Suppose they should give her a new complexion? Make her quite well again? Wouldn't that be worth while?"

Dot held the really dreadful looking doll away from her and gazed with loving eyes upon the wreck of her former pink and white beauty.

"She is just as—as dear to me as ever she was," she sighed. "But I s'pose her complexion is muddy—and her nose is flattened a little—and her lips aren't red any more--and her eyes are washed out. But—but are you sure they won't hurt her?"

"We'll have to find a hospital where they agree not to hurt," said Neale seriously.

"Now you've got yourself in a mess, Neale O 'Neil," whispered Agnes. "She'll never let you rest."

But the boy only grinned at her. Tess came back. Ruth brought the hats of Agnes and herself and their outer wraps. Everything that they could possibly need for the day's outing was gathered together and taken out to the big, shiny, seven-passenger touring car that stood gloriously in the morning sunshine before the Willow Street door of the old Corner House.

Tom Jonah, the old Newfoundland dog, and the guardian of the premises, evidently desired to accompany the merry party; but Ruth vetoed that, although he might have ridden in the front seat with Neale.

"And I'm going to ride there myself," declared Agnes, firmly. "I've got to learn to run this car right away. If Neale could learn, and get a license, Ican. By the way, Neale, where is your license?"

"Oh, I've got it with me," returned the boy. "D' you want me to have it pasted on the back of my coat?"

"Tom Jonah must stay at home—and the kittens, too," said Tess, looking at the troop of cats and kittens lingering about the side porch, waiting for their morning meal.

"And Billy Bumps," added Dot, referring to the solemn old goat grazing on the drying green.

Uncle Rufus, the black factotum of the Corner House, came up from the garden, grinning widely at them.

"Don' yo' chillun run down nothin'—nor run up nothin'—w'ile yo' is gone. I dunno 'bout dat contraption. Ah hopes yo' git back widout more'n a dozen laigs broke."

"Goodness, Uncle Rufus!" cried Agnes. "What do you think we are—centipedes?"

"Dunno nottin' 'bout dem 'er," declared the old colored man, chuckling. "Don't hab center-pigs in Virginny, whar I done come from. Dey uses razorbacks fo' de mos' part in makin' po'k."

The car started amid a gale of laughter at this. Mrs. MacCall waved her cap from an open second story window. Some of the neighbors took a deep interest in their departure, too. It was certainly a fact that the Corner House girls had suddenly become of much importance since it was known that they had a car.

Ruth and the others looked up at Aunt Sarah Maltby's windows at the front of the house as the car jounced delightfully across the tracks on Main Street. But the old lady kept her curtains drawn. She would not even look out at them.

They sped along so easily, the strong springs and shock-absorbers taking the jar at the crossings, that even Ruth sighed ecstatically. Agnes murmured:

"This is life. Oh, Neale! it's the most delightful way to travel."

"Is it better than riding horses in a circus, Neale?" demanded Tess, from the tonneau.

Neale laughed. He had been circus born and bred, and the little girls still believed that such a life must be one round of pleasure and excitement. They never could understand why Neale had run away from Twomley & Sorber's Herculean Circus and Menagerie.

Suddenly Agnes, the volatile, thought of another thing. "Oh, me! Oh, my!" she cried. "What ever should we do?"

"Goodness! what's the matter with you now?" demanded her older sister.

"Suppose our auto should be stolen like Mr. Collinger's!"

"Don't say that, Aggie!" wailed Tess.

"They couldn't steal our auto," declared Dot, with emphasis.

"Why not?" asked Neale, curiously.

"'Cause Tom Jonah wouldn't let 'em," said the smallest girl.

"Then we should have brought Tom Jonah with us," Agnes said. "We'll have to let him watch the car all the time."

"Mr. Collinger's car was taken right away from the front of the County Court House. Those thieves were bold," said Ruth. "I heard Mr. Howbridge say that there was something behind that affair. He doubts if the car was stolen by any common thieves."

"Common or uncommon," cried Agnes, "we don't want ours stolen!"

"Better set a watch at the garage door at night," chuckled Neale.

They were out in the country now and had entered a smooth, but "woodsy," road that passed through a rather thick forest. The road was very narrow in places and there were only a few houses along the track for some miles.

Suddenly they sighted just ahead a basket phaeton and a brown, fat pony hitched to it. Neale slowed down quickly, for the turnout was standing still. The driver was a middle-aged woman with a good many fussy looking ribbons in her bonnet and otherwise dressed quite gaily. The fat brown pony was standing still, flicking flies with his tail and wagging his ears comfortably. He was in the very middle of the road and by no possibility could the car be steered around the turnout.

The woman looked around at the car and its passengers and her face displayed a most exasperated expression.

"I don't know what you'll do!" she cried, in a rather shrill voice. "I can't make him budge. He's been standing here this way for fifteen minutes, and sometimes he balks for hours!"

CHAPTER II—WHAT MRS. HEARD HEARD

"Can't you back, Neale?" asked Ruth Kenway, doubtfully. "We really don't want to stay here all day."

"Or wait upon the pleasure of a ridiculous beast like that," snapped Agnes, more than a little exasperated herself.

The woman looked around again. She had a pleasant face, and Tess smiled at her. Tess knew that the lady must feel a good deal worse than they did about it.

"You don't know how ridiculous he is," said the woman, hopelessly. "He may start any minute; then again he may stay here until he gets hungry. And he's only just eaten his breakfast."

"He looks as if he'd live as long without eating as a camel can go without drinking," chuckled Neale O'Neil.

"It's no laughing matter," protested Agnes. "We want to get somewhere."

"You can't want to get somewhere worse than I do, my dear," said the woman, with a sigh. "And only think! I have sat behind this pony hours and hours during the past ten years."

"Can't—can't he be cured?" asked Tess, doubtfully.

"He's a real pretty pony, I think," said Dot.

"'Handsome is as handsome does,' Mrs. Mac would say," Ruth declared. "Is there no way of turning, Neale?" she repeated.

"I don't see how. We don't want to scratch the car all up in those bushes and on those stumps. And if we back to where the road is wider we'll have to back for half a mile."

"A trolley car is lots better than an auto, then," declared Dot, with conviction.

"Why, Dottie! how can you say that?" cried Tess, in utter disapproval.

"'Cause if it gets stuck the motorman can go to the back end and run it just as well as at the front end," said the smallest Corner House girl, promptly.

"Some kid that!" murmured Neale, while the others laughed. "Have you tried the whip, ma'am?" he asked of the woman in the basket phaeton.

"I've broken it on him," confessed the woman, shaking her head. "He doesn't even feel it. The flies bother him more than a whip. He is just the most tantalizing brute of a horse that ever was. Jonas! Get up!"

Jonas stood still. He merely flicked flies and wagged his ears. He was really the most peaceful animate object visible in the whole landscape.

The Corner House girls, since coming to Milton to live in the old dwelling that Uncle Peter Stower had left them at his death, had enjoyed many adventures, but few more ridiculous than this. Here they sat in their new, high-powered car, ready and anxious to spin over the country roads to their goal—a famous picnicking grounds fifty miles from Milton—and a little old fat brown pony, with a stubborn disposition and a cropped mane, held them up as certainly as though he had been a highway robber!

The four young Kenways—Ruth, Agnes, Tess and Dot—with Aunt Sarah Maltby (who really was only an "adopted" aunt) had been very poor indeed before Uncle Peter Stower had died and left the girls the bulk of his estate and a small legacy to Aunt Sarah.

Mr. Howbridge, the administrator of the estate and the girls' guardian, had come to the Kenways' poor tenement in the city where they lived, and had taken them to the old Corner House—quite an old mansion overlooking the Parade Ground in Milton, and supposed by some of the neighbors to be "haunted."

How the girls laid the "garret ghost" and how they proved their right and title to Uncle Peter's estate against the claims of a certain Mrs. Treble (known as "Mrs. Trouble" to the rather pert Agnes) and her little girl, "Double-Trouble," is told in the first volume of this series, entitled "The Corner House Girls."

Afterward the little "Adamless Eden" on the corner of Willow and Main Streets is trespassed upon by a boy who has run away from a circus to get an education—Neale O'Neil. He proves to be a thoroughly likable boy, and even Ruth and Tess, who do not much approve of the opposite sex, are prone to like Neale.

In "The Corner House Girls at School" Neale becomes a fixture in the neighborhood, living with Mr. Con Murphy, the little old cobbler on the street back of the Stower place, and doing chores for the Corner House girls and other neighbors to help support himself while he attends school.

The girls extend their acquaintance widely during this first school year at Milton, and when summer comes they visit Pleasant Cove, where they befriend Rosa and June Wildwood, two Southern girls, and meanwhile have adventures galore along the shore. Indeed, "The Corner House Girls Under Canvas" introduces many new friends to both the girls themselves and to the reader, notable among whom is Tom Jonah, who, although only a dog, is a thorough gentleman.

The girls' friendliness to all living creatures gathers about them, as is natural, a galaxy of pets, including a rapidly growing menagerie of cats, the dog in question, a goat, and (this is Agnes' inclusion) Sammy Pinkney, the little boy who is determined to be a pirate when he grows up.

The fall following this summer vacation just mentioned, sees all the Corner House girls taking part in a play produced by the combined effort of the town schools. Their failures and successes in producing The Carnation Countess is interwoven with a mystery surrounding the punishment of Agnes and some of her fellow-classmates for an infraction of the rules—a punishment that promises at one time to spoil the play entirely. "The Corner House Girls in a Play" is interesting and it turns out happily in the end. One of the best things about it is the fact that three thousand dollars is raised by means of the play for the Women's and Children's Hospital, and Mrs. Eland, the matron, is able to retain her position in that institution.

Mrs. Eland and her sister, Miss Pepperill, who has been Tess Kenway's school teacher, become very good friends of the Corner House girls. In the volume of the series immediately preceding this present narrative, entitled "The Corner House Girls' Odd Find" the Kenways find an old, apparently worthless, album in the garret of the mansion—a treasure room which seems inexhaustible in its supply of mystery and amusing incidents.

This album seems to contain a lot of counterfeit money and bonds, which in the end prove to have been hidden in the Stower house by a miserly uncle of Mrs. Eland and Miss Pepperill, Mr. Lemuel Aden, who had died too suddenly to make a will or to tell of his hidden treasure—and the money and bonds are really perfectly good.

The four Kenway sisters, therefore, saw their friends, the hospital matron and the school teacher, made comfortably wealthy for life; and the beautiful, seven passenger touring car, with self-starter, "quick top," and all the modern appurtenances of a good automobile, was the gift of the legatees of Mr. Lemuel Aden.

"But it might as well be a flivver," said Agnes, in disgust, "if we've got to sit here all day and watch a fat brown pony whisk his tail."

"I don't see what I can do, my dear," said the woman in the basket phaeton. "You can't lead him, and you can't push him, and I verily believe if you built a fire under him he'd just move up far enough to burn the cart, and stand there until his harness scorched him."

Agnes giggled at that, and was her own jolly self again. "It's up to you, Neale O'Neil," she declared. "You're the chauffeur and are supposed to make us go. Make us!"

"Get out and walk around the pony," proposed Neale, grinning.

"And what about the car?"

"Do you think we could lift it over?" said Ruth, with scorn.

"Now, young man," Agnes pursued, with gravity. "It is your duty to get us to Marchenell Grove. We're still twenty-five or thirty miles away from it——"

"My goodness!" exclaimed the lady in front. "Were you young folks going there?"

"We had an idea of doing so when we started, ma'am," said Agnes, quickly.

"I should have gone there to-day, too——"

"Not with that pony?" shrieked Agnes, clasping her hands.

"Why—no," said the lady, smiling. "But if my nephew hadn't lost his automobile he would have taken me. Oh, dear! Now I shall have to ride behind Jonas all the time."

"You really don't call this riding, do you, ma'am?" asked the irrepressible Agnes.

The woman laughed. She liked Agnes Kenway from the first, as almost everybody who met her did.

"I'm not riding fast just now, and that's a fact," she said, nodding her bonnet with its many bows. "Nor does Jonas take me over the roads very rapidly at his very best pace."

Neale O'Neil had got slowly out of the car and now walked around to the head of the fat brown pony. The pony had blue eyes, and they were very mild. But he seemed to have no idea of going on and getting himself and his mistress out of the way of the automobile. Maybe he did not like automobiles.

"You see, my nephew bought a car and we let Jonas kick up his heels in the paddock. Oh! he's lively enough when he wants to be—Jonas, I mean. But my nephew's car was stolen day before yesterday—and he's worried almost to death about it, poor man."

"Oh!" cried Ruth, "who is your nephew, Madam?"

"Why, Philip Collinger is my nephew. He's the county surveyor, you know. A very bright young man—if I do say it. But not bright enough to keep from having his auto stolen," she added, ruefully.

Just then Agnes, who had been watching Neale O'Neil, called:

"What are you doing to that pony, Neale?"

The boy had rubbed the fat brown pony's nose. He had lifted first one foot and then the other, going all around the pony to do so. He had patted his neck. Jonas had seemed rather to like these attentions. He still whisked flies calmly.

Now Neale reached over and took one of the pony's ears in his hand, holding it firmly. To the other ear the boy put his lips and seemed to be whispering something privately to Jonas.

"What are you doing to that pony, Neale?" cried Agnes again.

"Mercy! what is the boy doing? Why, Jonas doesn't pay any attention to me when I fairly yell at him. He's deaf, I believe."

And then the lady stopped, startled. The four Corner House girls all expressed their amazement with a united cry. Neale had taken the pony firmly by the bridle and was leading him quietly out of the middle of the road.

"For pity's sake!" gasped the pony's mistress, "I never saw the like of that before."

Jonas seemed to have forgotten all about balking. He still wagged his ears to keep the flies away and whisked his tail industriously.

Neale, leading the pony, turned a corner in the lane, and there came upon a house. The lady had left the phaeton to speak to the girls more companionably. Neale tied the pony to the picket fence before the house, leaving the hitching strap long enough to allow the animal to graze.

"Well, I want to know!" cried the woman, when the boy returned to the car. "How did you do that? What did you do to Jonas to make him change his mind?"

"This is Mrs. Heard, Neale," said Ruth, smiling. "You sometimes do prove to be a smart boy. What did you do to him?"

Neale grinned broadly. He had been used to horses all his life and he knew a few tricks of the Gypsies and the horse-traders.

"I just told him something," the boy said.

"Oo-ee!" cried Tess. "Did you really whisper to him?"

Neale nodded.

"What did you whisper to the pony?" asked Dot, wide-eyed.

Agnes snapped, thinking Neale was fooling her: "I don't believe it!"

"Yes, I whispered to him," said the boy, seriously.

"Oh, Neale!" remonstrated Ruth.

"Well! For all I ever heard!" exclaimed Mrs. Heard. "What did you whisper to that vexatious brute of a pony?"

"If I told what it was, that would spoil the charm," said Neale, gravely.

"Nonsense!" ejaculated Agnes, flushing.

"Now you know that is ridiculous," said Ruth, inclined to be exasperated with the boy as much as she had been with the pony.

"No. It is a fact," said the boy, decidedly.

"Now, you know that isn't so, Neale O'Neil!" cried Agnes.

"I assure you it is. Anyway, they say if you tell it—what you say—to anybody else, the horse will balk again right away. It's a secret between him and the person——"

"I never heard such a ridiculous thing in all my life," gasped Mrs. Heard.

"I think you are not very polite, Neale," said Ruth, quite sternly.

"Now see here!" cried the badgered boy, getting rather vexed himself. "I tell you I can't tell you——"

"You're talking anything but English," complained Agnes.

"Well, maybe I didn't talk English into the pony's ear," retorted Neale, grinning suddenly again. "Anyway, the old Gyp who taught me that trick told me I must never say the words aloud, or to anybody who would not make proper use of the magic formula."

"Oh, shucks!" exclaimed Agnes, in disgust. "Tell me. I'll try it on Billy Bumps when he balks," said Tess, in a small voice.

At that they all laughed and Neale got in behind the steering wheel again. The two older girls were much interested in Mrs. Heard and that woman was evidently pleased with the sisters.

"Why, yes; I ought to know you Corner House girls. Goodness knows I've heard enough about you—and my name being Heard, I heard a lot!" and she laughed. "But you see, I live away on this side of town, and don't go to your church; so we have never met before."

"I am sure the loss has been ours," said Ruth, politely. "I hope your pony will not balk again to-day."

"Goodness knows! He'll balk if he takes a notion to. I don't suppose what you whispered to him is guaranteed to be a permanent cure, is it, boy?" she asked Neale O'Neil.

"No, ma'am," grinned the boy.

"And you expected to go to Marchenell Grove to-day, Mrs. Heard?" Ruth said, reflectively, looking at Agnes enquiringly although she spoke to the mistress of the fat brown pony.

"I had thought to. Philly Collinger was going to take me. But if he doesn't recover his car he'll not take me auto riding very soon again."

"Well," said Ruth, having received a nod of acquiescence from Agnes, "I don't see why you shouldn't go there to-day just the same. Won't you come with us? There's room in the car."

"Goody! Of course she can!" cried Agnes, clapping her hands.

"I think that would be real nice," agreed Tess.

Dot moved over at once to make room. "She can sit beside me and the Alice-doll," she proclaimed.

"Well, I declare!" exclaimed Mrs. Heard, her face alight with pleasure at this united invitation. "You are just the nicest girls I ever met. I wonder if I'd better?"

"Of course," said Ruth. "You can find some place to leave the pony. Or Neale can, I'm sure."

"Why, I know these people right in the very next house," said Mrs. Heard. "Indeed I expected to call there if Jonas ever got that far."

Neale got briskly out of the car again. "I'll go and unharness him," he said, cheerfully. "You just find out where I shall put him. He'd rather have you ride in an automobile than drag you himself," and he laughed.

"Did—did he tell you so, Neale, when you were talking with him?" asked Dot, in amazement.

Then they all laughed.

CHAPTER III—WHAT MRS. HEARD TOLD

In ten minutes the Kenway car was moving again. Jonas had been put up at the barn of Mrs. Heard's friends, near which the pony had balked, and Neale soon whisked them out of sight of the place.

"This—this is just delightful," sighed Mrs. Heard. "Especially after sitting behind that brute of a pony. I do love an automobile."

"So do I!" Agnes cried. "I'd rather ride in this car than in a golden chariot—I know I would."

"I don't know how they run chariots, nowadays," said Neale, chuckling; "whether by horse-power or gas. But sometimes a car balks, you know."

"Not so often as that Jonas," declared Mrs. Heard. "I've been out with my nephew a lot. His is a nice car. I hope he'll find it."

"Why, of course the thieves will be apprehended," said Ruth. "What good are the police?"

"When it comes to autos," said Neale, slyly, "the police are mostly good for stopping you and getting you fined."

"Well, don't you dare drive too fast and get us fined, Neale O'Neil," ordered Ruth, sternly.

"No, ma'am," he returned. But Agnes whispered in his ear:

"I don't care how fast you run it, Neale. I love to go fast."

"You'll be a speed fiend, Aggie," he declared. "That's what you'll be."

"Oh! I want to drive. I must learn."

"You'll have to ask Mr. Howbridge about that," Neale told her.

"Oh!"

"Yes, ma'am! He told me that I shouldn't allow anybody to run the car but a properly qualified person."

"You don't mean it?" gasped the eager girl.

"That's right! A person with a license."

"I can't believe it, Neale O'Neil!" wailed Agnes. "How am I ever going to learn, then?"

"You'll have to go to the garage as I did and take lessons."

Agnes pouted over this. Mrs. Heard, meanwhile, was saying to Ruth:

"Yes, the stealing of my nephew's auto was an outrage. Politics in this county are most disgraceful. If we women voted——"

"But, Mrs. Heard! what have politics to do with your nephew's auto being stolen?" cried Ruth.

"Oh! it wasn't any ordinary thief, or perhaps thieves, who took his car. He is sure of that. You see, there are some politicians who want the plans and maps of the new road surveys his office has been making."

"What sort of maps are those?" asked Tess, who was listening. "Like those we have to outline in the geography?"

"They are not like those, chicken," laughed Ruth. "They are outlines—drawings. They show the road levels and grades. I guess you don't understand. Don't you remember those men who came the other day and looked through instruments on our sidewalk and measured with a long tape line, and all that?"

"Oh, yes," confessed Tess. "I saw them."

"Well, they were surveyors. And they were working for Mr. Collinger, I suppose," said Ruth.

"Oh!"

"I saw them, too," proclaimed Dot. "I thought they were photo—photographers. I went out there and stood with my Alice-doll right in front of one of those things on the three sticks."

"You did?" cried Agnes, who heard this. "What for, Dottums?"

"To get our picture tooken," said Dot, gravely. "And then I asked the man when it would be done and if we could see a picture."

"Ho, ho!" laughed Neale O'Neil. "What did he say?"

"Why," confessed the smallest Corner House girl, indignantly, "he said I'd be grown up—and so would Alice—before that picture was enveloped——"

"'Developed'!" cried Tess.

"No. Enveloped," said Dot, stoutly. "You always get photograph proofs in an envelope."

Ruth and Mrs. Heard were laughing heartily. Agnes said, admiringly:

"You're a wonder, Dot! If there is a possible way of fumbling a thing, you do it."

The little girls were not likely to understand all that Mrs. Heard said about the disappearance of Mr. Collinger's automobile—no more than Dot understood about the surveyor's transit. But they listened.

"You understand, Miss Ruth," said the aunt of the county surveyor, "that Phil Collinger is responsible for all those tracings and maps that are being made in this road survey.

"If it gets out just what changes are to be made in grades and routes through the county before the commission renders its report, there is a chance for some of these 'pauper politicians,' as Philly calls them, to make money."

"I don't see how," said Agnes, putting her oar in. "What good would the maps do even dishonest people?"

"Because with foreknowledge of the highway commission's determinations, men could go and get options upon property adjoining the highways that will be changed, and either sell to the county at a big profit or hold abutting properties for the natural rise in land values that will follow."

"I understand what an option is," said Ruth. "It is a small sum which a man pays down on a place, with the privilege of buying it at a stated price within a given length of time."

"You talk just like a judge, Ruthie," giggled Agnes. "For my part I don't understand it at all. But I'm sorry Mr. Collinger lost his car."

"And it was stolen so boldly," said Neale, shaking his head.

"But why did they steal the car, Mrs. Heard?" demanded Ruth, sticking to the main theme. "What has that to do with the surveyors' maps?"

"Why," said the lady, slowly, "they must have seen Philly come out of the court house and throw a package into the car. He covered it with a robe. They knew—or supposed they knew—that he carried the maps around with him. He could not even trust the safe in his office. It's no better than a tin can and could be opened with a hammer and chisel."

"Oh, my!" exclaimed Agnes, interested again. "So they stole the car to get the maps? Just like a moving picture play, isn't it?"

"Maybe it is," sighed the lady. "But it is quite serious for Philly—whether they got the maps or not."

"Oh! Didn't they?" cried Ruth.

"That—that he won't say," said Mrs. Heard, shaking her head. "I'm sure I don't know. Philly Collinger can be just as close-mouthed as an oyster—and so I tell him.

"But everybody thinks the maps were in that package he put in the car before he ran across the street to get a bite of lunch. And I'm pretty sure that he isn't worried all that much over the stealing of his car. Though goodness knows when he can ever afford to buy another. The salary of surveyor in this county isn't a fortune.

"So, there it is," said Mrs. Heard. "The car's gone, and I guess the maps and data are gone with it. Somebody, of course, hired the two scamps that took it to do the trick——"

"Oh, were there two?" asked Neale, who had been running the car slowly again in order to listen.

"Yes. They were seen; but nobody supposed they were stealing the car, of course."

"What kind of men were they? How did they look?" asked Agnes.

"What do you want to know for, Miss Detective?" chuckled Neale.

"So as to be on the watch for them. If I see one of them about our car, I shall make a disturbance," announced the beauty, with decision.

"I don't know much about them," admitted Mrs. Heard, laughing with the others over Agnes' statement. "But one was a young man with a fancy band on his straw hat and yellow freckles on his face. I believe he had a little mustache. But he might shave that," she added, reflectively.

"And change the band on his hat," whispered Neale to Agnes, his eyes dancing.

"Never mind about his hat-band, Neale O'Neil!" cried Agnes, standing up suddenly in a most disconcerting way. "What is that ahead?"

Neale promptly shut off the power and braked. Agnes was greatly excited, and she pointed to a place in the road not many yards in advance.

The way was narrow, with rocky fields on either side approached by rather steep banks. Indeed, the road lay through what might well be called a ravine. It was the worst piece of road, too (so the guidebook, said), of any stretch between Milton and Marchenell Grove.

As the car stopped, Neale saw what Agnes had seen. Right across the way—directly in front of the automobile—lay something long and iridescent. It was moving.

"Oh!" shrieked Agnes again. "It's a snake—a horrid, great, big snake!"

"Well, what under the sun did you make me stop for?" demanded the boy. "I'd have gone right over it."

"That would have been cruel, boy," declared Mrs. Heard, from behind.

"Cruel? Huh! It's a rattler," returned Neale.

"Oh, Neale! It's never!" gasped Agnes, not meaning to be impolite.

"A rattler, Neale?" asked Ruth. "Are you sure?"

"What's a rattler?" asked Dot, composedly. "Is it what they make baby's rattles out of?"

"Mercy, no!" shivered Tess. "Neale means it's a rattlesnake."

"Oh! I don't like them," declared Dot, immediately picking up the Alice-doll, of which she always first thought in time of peril.

"What shall we do?" demanded Ruth.

"Can't he drive around it?" asked Mrs. Heard, rather excitedly. "I don't believe at all in hurting any dumb animal—not even a snake or a spider."

"How about breaking the whip on old Jonas?" whispered Neale to Agnes.

But his girl friend was all of a shiver. "Do get around it, Neale," she begged.

"Can't. The road's too narrow," declared the boy, with promptness. "And I am bound to run over the thing if it doesn't move out of the way. I can't help it."

"Wait!" cried Mrs. Heard. "Get out and poke it with a stick."

"Why, Mrs. Heard!" exclaimed Ruth, "do you realize that a rattlesnake is deadly poison? I wouldn't let Neale do such a thing."

"Besides being a suffragist," declared Mrs. Heard, firmly, "I am a professing and acting member of the S.P.C.A. I cannot look on and see a harmless beast—it is not doing anything to us—wantonly killed or injured."

"Good-night!" murmured Neale.

Just then the snake—and it was a big fellow, all of six feet long—seemed to awaken. Perhaps it had been chilled by the coolness of the night before; it was lethargic, at any rate.

It lifted its head, whirled into the very middle of the road, and faced the automobile defiantly. In a moment it had coiled and sprung its rattle. The whirring sound, once heard, is never to be mistaken for any other.

"Oh, dear! what shall we do?" gasped Agnes. "If you try to run over it, it may get into the car—or something," said Ruth.

The roadway was narrower here than it had been back where the brown pony had held the party up. This first trip in their automobile seemed to be fraught with much adventure for the Corner House girls and Neale O'Neil.

CHAPTER IV—SALERATUS JOE

Neale O'Neil knew very well that he could not satisfy everybody—least of all the rattlesnake.

Mrs. Heard did not want her S.P.C.A. sensibilities hurt; Agnes wanted him to drive on; Ruth wished him to dodge the coiled rattler. As for getting out and "coaxing it to move on" with a stick, Neale had no such intention.

He tried starting slowly to see if the serpent would be frightened and open the way for the passage of the car. But the rattler instantly coiled and sprang twice at the hood. The second time it sank its fangs into the left front tire.

"Cricky!" gasped Neale. "They say you swell all up when one of those things injects poison into you; but I don't believe that tire will swell any more than it is."

"Don't make fun!" groaned Agnes. "Suppose it should jump into the car?"

"If we only had a gun," began Neale.

"Well, I hope you haven't, young man," cried Mrs. Heard. "I'm deadly afraid of firearms."

"Don't get out of the car, Neale," begged Agnes, clasping her hands.

"Try to back away from it," suggested Ruth.

The smaller girls clung to each other (Dot determinedly to the Alice-doll, as well), and, although they did not say much, they were frightened. Tess whispered:

"Oh, dear me! I'm 'fraid enough of the wriggling fish-worms that Sammy digs in our garden. And this snake is a hundred times as big!"

"And fish-worms don't shoot people with their tongues, do they?" suggested Dot.

Just at that very moment, when the six-foot rattler had coiled to strike again, there was a rattling and jangling of tinware from up the road. There was a turn not far ahead, and the young folks could not see beyond it.

"Goodness me!" exploded Agnes, "what's coming now?"

"Not another rattlesnake, I bet a cent—though it's some rattling," chuckled Neale O'Neil.

The heads of a pair of horses then appeared around the turn. They proved to be drawing a tin-peddler's wagon, and over this rough piece of driveway the wash-boilers, dishpans, kettles, pails, and a dozen other articles of tin and agate-ware, were making more noise than the passage of a battery of artillery.

Some scientists have pointed out that snakes—some snakes, at least—seem to be hard of hearing. That could not have been so with the big rattlesnake that had held up the Kenways and their automobile.

Before the Jewish peddler on the seat of the wagon could draw his willing horses to a halt, the snake swiftly uncoiled and wriggled across the road and into the bushes. All that was left to mark his recent presence was a wavy mark in the dust.

"Vat's the madder?" called the peddler. "Ain't dere room to ged by?"

"Sure," said the relieved Neale. "Let me back a little and you pull out to the right, and we'll be all right. We were held up by a snake."

The Jew (he was a little man with fiery hair and whiskers, and he had a narrow-brimmed derby hat jammed down upon his head), seemed to study over this answer of the boy for fully a minute. Then, as Neale was steering the automobile slowly past his rig, he leaned sidewise and asked, with a broad smile:

"I say, mister! Vat did you say stopped you?"

"A snake," declared Neale, grinning.

"Oy, oy! And that it iss yedt to drive one of them so benzine carts? No! Mein horses iss petter. They are not afraid of snakes."

He still sat, without starting his team, thinking the surprising matter over, when the automobile turned the curve in the road and struck better going.

"Well!" ejaculated Agnes, "I only hope he stays there till that snake comes out of the bushes again and climbs into his cart."

"My! how disagreeable you can be," returned Neale, laughing. "I don't believe you'll get your wish, however."

"I'm glad we didn't run over that snake," declared Mrs. Heard, nodding her head. "I'm opposed to killing any dumb creature."

"Then," suggested Dot, earnestly, "you must be like Mr. Seneca Sprague."

"Me? Like Seneca Sprague?" gasped the lady, yet rather amused. "I like that!"

"Why, how can that be, Dot?" asked Ruth, rather puzzled herself, for Seneca Sprague was a queer character who was thought by most Milton people to be a little crazy.

"Why, he's a vegetablearian. And Mrs. Heard must be," announced Dot, confidently, "if she doesn't believe in killing dumb beasts."

"There's logic for you!" exclaimed Neale. "Score one for Dot."

The lady laughed heartily. "I suppose I ought to be a 'vegetablearian' if I'm not," she said. "I dunno as I could worship beasts the way some of the ancients did; but I don't believe in killing them unnecessarily."

"I know about some of the animal gods and goddesses the Greeks and Egyptians used to worship," ventured Tess, who had not taken much part in the conversation of late. "Did any of them worship snakes, do you s'pose?"

"I believe some peoples did," Ruth told her.

"Oh, I know about gods and goddesses," cried Dot, eagerly. "Our teacher read about them—or, some of them—only yesterday, in school."

"Well, Miss Know-it-all," said Agnes, good-naturedly, "what did you learn about them?"

"I—I remember 'bout one named Ceres," said the smallest Corner House girl, with corrugated brow, trying to remember what she had heard read.

"Well, what about her?" asked Agnes, encouragingly.

"What was Ceres the goddess of, honey?" pursued Ruth, as Dot still hesitated.

"Why—why she was the goddess of dressmaking," declared the child, with sudden conviction.

"Oh, oh, oh!" ejaculated Neale, under his breath.

"For goodness sake! where did you get that idea?" demanded Ruth, while Agnes and Mrs. Heard positively could not keep from laughing, and Tess looked at her smaller sister with something like horror. "Why—Dot Kenway!" she murmured.

"She is, too!" pouted Dot. "My teacher said so. She said Ceres was the goddess of 'ripping and sewing.' Now, isn't that dressmaking?"

"Oh, cricky!" gasped Neale, and swerved the car to the left in his emotion.

"Do be careful, Neale!" squealed Agnes.

"Yes. You'll have us into something," warned Ruth.

"Then put ear-muffs on me," groaned the boy. "That child will be the death of me yet. 'Sowing and reaping'—'ripping and sewing'—wow!"

"Humph!" observed Agnes. "You needn't be the death of us if she does say something funny. Do keep your mind on what you are about, Neale."

But Neale O'Neil was a careful driver. He was a sober boy, anyway, and would never qualify in the joy-riding class, that was sure.

The remainder of the ride to Marchenell Grove was a jolly and enjoyable one. They all liked Mrs. Heard more and more as they became better acquainted with her. She seemed to know just how to get along with young folk, and despite her stated suffragist and S.P.C.A. proclivities, even Neale pronounced her "good fun."

The Grove was a very popular resort, and very large. Perhaps it was just as well that Mrs. Heard was with the girls, for unexpectedly a situation developed during the day that might have been really unpleasant had not an older person—like the good and talkative lady—been with them.

There was a large party of picnickers that had come together and that made one end of the grounds very lively. There was an orchestra with them and they usurped the dancing pavilion. Not that Ruth or Agnes would have danced here; neither Mr. Howbridge nor Mrs. MacCall would have approved; nor did Mrs. Heard countenance dancing in such a public place. But after they had all been out in boats on the river, and had eaten their lunch, and enjoyed the swings, and strolled through the pleasant paths of the Grove, it was only natural that the two older Kenways should wish to see the dancing. They had no idea that the crowd about the pavilion was rowdyish.

Neale was busy with the car in preparation for their return to Milton. The little girls were watching him at work, and Mrs. Heard was resting in the car, too. So Ruth and Agnes went alone down to the pavilion.

"Dear me," sighed Agnes. "I really wish we could have just one spin on the floor—just us two. That music makes my feet fairly itch."

"You will have to possess your soul with patience—or else scratch your poor little feet," laughed her sister. "To think of your wanting to dance here! I am afraid all these people—especially the boys—are not nice."

"I don't care. I don't want to dance with them," pouted Agnes. "Only with you. I just love to dance to this piece the orchestra is playing."

"Save it till next week's school dance," laughed Ruth. "Oh!"

Her startled ejaculation was brought out by the appearance of a strange young man at her elbow. He was really not a nice looking fellow at all, his face was unpleasantly freckled, and the corners of his lips and the ends of the first three fingers of his right hand were stained deeply by the use of cigarettes.

"Aft'noon!" said this stranger, affably. "Want a whirl? The floor's fine—come on in."

Agnes, who was much more timid in reality than she usually appeared, shrank from the fellow, trying to draw Ruth with her.

"Let the kid wait for us," suggested the freckled young man, leering good-naturedly enough at Agnes, and probably not at all aware that he was distasteful to the Kenway girls. "We can have one whirl."

"I am much obliged to you," Ruth said, rather falteringly. "I would rather not."

"Aw, say—just a turn. Don't throw me down," said the fellow, his eyes becoming suddenly hard and the smile beginning to disappear from his face.

"No, thank you. Neither my sister nor I wish to dance here," said Ruth, growing bolder—and more indignant.

"Don't tell me you don't know how to dance?" growled the freckled one.

"I don't tell you anything, but that we do not wish to dance," and Ruth tried to turn away from him.

The fellow stepped directly in their path. They were just on the fringe of loiterers about the pavilion. Agnes clapped a hand upon her lips to keep from screaming.

"Aw, come on," said the fellow, laying a detaining hand upon Ruth's arm.

Then something very unexpected, but very welcome, happened. Mrs. Heard, seeing a hand's breadth of cloud in the sky and fearing a thunder storm, had sent Neale O'Neil scurrying for the girls. He came to the spot before this affair could go any farther.

"Hullo!" he exclaimed, sharply. "What's this?"

"This—this gentleman," said Ruth, faintly, "offers to dance with me, but I tell him 'no.'"

"What are you butting in for, kid?" demanded the freckled young fellow, thrusting his jaw forward in an ugly manner. But he took his hand from Ruth's arm.

Neale said to the girls, quite quietly though his eyes flashed:

"Mrs. Heard wants you to come back to the car at once. Please hurry."

"Say! I don't get you," began the rough again.

"You will in a moment," Neale shot at him. "Go away, girls!"

Agnes did not want to go now; but Ruth saw it would be better and she fairly dragged her sister away.

"Neale will be hurt!" moaned Agnes, all the way to the car. "That awful rowdy has friends, of course."

What really happened to Neale the girls never knew, for he would not talk about it. Trained from his very babyhood as an acrobat, the ex-circus boy would be able to give a good account of himself if it came to fisticuffs with the freckled-faced fellow. Although the latter was considerably older and taller than Neale, the way he had lived had not hardened his muscles and made him quick of eye and foot or handy with his fists.

Perhaps Neale did not fight at all. At least he came back to the car without a mark upon him and without even having had his clothes ruffled. All he said in answer to the excited questions of the girls was:

"That's a fellow called Saleratus Joe. You can tell why—his face with all those yellow freckles looks like an old fashioned saleratus biscuit. He belongs in Milton. I've seen him before. He isn't much better than a saloon lounger."

"Goodness me!" exclaimed Mrs. Heard. "Saleratus Joe is one of the fellows who my nephew thinks stole his automobile. I must tell him that we saw the fellow. Perhaps the car can be traced after all."

"Through Saleratus Joe?" said Neale O'Neil. "Well—maybe."

CHAPTER V—DOT'S AWFUL ADVENTURE

Altogether that first run in their automobile was pronounced a jolly success by the Corner House girls. The return journey from Marchenell Grove was without incident.

"If we had only become acquainted with Mrs. Heard the trip would have been more than worth while," declared Ruth, who was seldom as enthusiastic about a new acquaintance as she was about the aunt of the county surveyor. "She is coming to see us soon."

Agnes was more interested in another thing, and she confided in Neale.

"Do you really suppose, Neale," she asked, "that the awful fellow who spoke to Ruth is one of those who stole Mr. Collinger's auto?"

"Saleratus Joe?" chuckled the boy.

"Hasn't he any other name? It sounds like—like the Wild West in the movies, or something like that."

"They only call him that for fun," explained Neale O'Neil. "And whether he helped get away with the surveyor's machine or not, I'm sure I don't know."

"But can't you guess?" cried Agnes, in exasperation.

"What's the use of guessing?" returned her boy chum. "That won't get you anywhere. You're a poor detective, Aggie."

"Don't make fun," complained Agnes, who was very much excited about the automobile robbery. They had just got their car, and she had longed for it so deeply that she was beginning to be worried for fear something would happen to it.

"Shut Tom Jonah into the garage at night," Neale suggested. "I warrant no thieves will take it."

Mr. Howbridge, while he was about it, had had a cement block garage built on the rear of the Stower premises facing Willow Street, for the housing of the Corner House girls' motor car.

"Mr. Collinger's auto was stolen right on the street," said Agnes, doubtfully.

"That's the worst of these flivvers," retorted Neale, with a grin. "People are apt to come along and pick 'em up absent-mindedly and go off with them. Say! have you heard the latest?"

"What about?" asked Agnes, dreamily.

"About the flivver. Do you know what the chickens say when one of 'em goes by?"

"No," declared the girl.

"Cheep! Cheep! Cheep!" mimicked the boy.

Agnes giggled. Then she said: "But Mr. Collinger's wasn't one of those cheap cars. It was a runabout; but it cost him a lot of money."

"But that freckled-faced young man, Neale—do you suppose he could be the one Mrs. Heard said was seen driving the stolen car away from the court house?"

"Why, how should I know?" demanded Neale. "I'm no seventh son of a seventh son."

"I wish we had seen a constable out there in the grove and had had him arrested."

"What for? On what charge?" cried Neale, wonderingly.

"Why, because he spoke to Ruth and me. Then he could be held while his record was looked up. Maybe Mr. Collinger could have recovered his car by that means."

"Cricky!" ejaculated the boy. "You've been reading the police court reports in the newspapers, I believe, Aggie."

"Well! that's what they do," declared the girl, confidently.

"Maybe so. But you couldn't have had the fellow arrested for speaking to you. You shouldn't have been around the dance floor if you wanted to escape that. But, perhaps that freckled rascal is one of the thieves, and maybe he can be traced. Mrs. Heard will tell her nephew and he will attend to it—no fear!"

"But it would be just great, Neale, if we could do something toward recovering the car and getting the thieves arrested," said Agnes who, as Neale often said, if she went into a thing, went into it all over!

They had not much time just then, however, to give to the mystery of the county surveyor's lost automobile. Final examinations were coming on and the closing of school would be the next week but one.

Even Dot was busy with school work, although she was not very far advanced in her studies; and during these last few days she was released from her classes in the afternoon earlier than the other Corner House girls.

Sometimes she walked toward Meadow Street, which was across town from the Corner House and in a poorer section of Milton, with some of her little school friends before coming home; and so she almost always met Sammy Pinkney loafing along Willow Street on returning.

Sammy did not go to school this term. Scarlet fever had left this would-be pirate so weak and pale that the physician had advised nothing but out-of-doors for him until autumn.

Sammy, in some ways, was a changed boy since his serious illness. He was much thinner and less robust looking, of course; but the changes in him were not all of a physical nature. For one thing, he was not so rough with his near-neighbors, the Corner House girls. They had been very kind to him while he was ill, and his mother was always singing their praises. Besides, the other boys being in school, Sammy was lonely and was only too glad as a usual thing to have even Dot to talk to or play with.

Dot was a little afraid of Sammy, even now, because of his past well-won reputation. And, too, his reiterated desire to be a pirate cast a glamor over his character that impressed the smallest Corner House girl.

One day she met him on Willow Street, some distance from the old Corner House. He was idly watching a man across the street who was moving along the sidewalk in a very odd way indeed.

The Kenways had lived in a very poor part of Bloomingsburg before coming to Milton, and there had been saloons in the neighborhood; but Dot had been very small, and if she had seen such a thing as an intoxicated man she had forgotten it. Near the Corner House there were no saloons, although the city of

Milton licensed many of those places. Dot had not before seen a man under the influence of liquor.

This unfortunate was not a poorly dressed man. Indeed, he was rather well appareled and normally might have been a very respectable citizen. But he was staggering from side to side of the walk, his head hanging and his stiff derby hat—by some remarkable power—sticking to his head, although it threatened to fall off at every jerk.

"Why—ee!" gasped the smallest Corner House girl, "what ever is the matter with that poor man, Sammy Pinkney, do you suppose?"

Sammy, trying to wrap his limbs about a fire-plug in emulation of a boa-constrictor, jerked out:

"Brick in his hat!"

"Oh! What?" murmured the puzzled Dot, eyeing the poor man wonderingly and clasping the Alice-doll closer.

Sammy grinned. He was a tantalizing urchin and loved to mystify the innocent Dot.

"He's carrying a brick in his hat," he repeated, with daring.

"Why—why——Doesn't he know it?" demanded the little girl.

"I guess nobody's told him yet," chuckled Sammy.

At that moment the intoxicated man just caught his hat from tumbling off by striking it with the palm of one hand and so settling it well down upon his ears again.

"Oh, my!" murmured the startled Dot. "It came pretty near falling out, didn't it?"

"He, he!" snickered Sammy.

"Do you suppose he wants to carry that brick in his hat?" asked Dot, seriously. "I shouldn't think he would."

"He don't know he's got it," said Sammy.

"Why doesn't somebody tell him?" demanded Dot. "The poor man! He'll surely fall down."

Sammy still snickered. Somebody should have spanked Sammy, right then and there!

"I don't care!" exclaimed Dot, more and more disturbed, "it doesn't seem nice—not at all. I think you ought to tell him, Sammy."

"Not me!"

"Well——" Dot looked all around. There was nobody else in sight just then. Willow Street was quite deserted.

"If you won't, then I must," declared the little girl, shouldering the obligation pluckily and starting across the street.

"Aw, Dot! Let him alone," muttered Sammy.

The young rascal was suddenly startled. He began to wonder what would happen to him if his mother learned that he had been trying to fool Dot Kenway in any such way as this.

"Come back!" he called after her.

"Sha'n't!" declared Dot, who could be stubborn when she wanted to be.

"Say! that man won't listen to you," insisted Sammy.

Dot kept right on. The man had halted, and was clinging to a tree box, his head hanging down. His face was very much flushed and his eyes were glassy.

"But I s'pose," thought Dot, "if I was carrying a brick in my hat it would make me sick, too."

"Mister!" she said to the man, stopping in the gutter and looking up at him.

"Huh? What's matter?" asked the man. His head jerked up and he looked all around to see who had spoken to him.

"Mister," said Dot, earnestly, "I—I hope you'll 'scuse me, but there's a brick in your hat. Sammy Pinkney says so. And I think if you take it out you'll feel ever so much better."

Sammy heard her. He actually grew pale, and, casting a startled glance around him, he ran. He ran all the way home, for he could not imagine what the man would say or do to Dot. Sammy was not a very brave boy.

The unfortunate man looked down at Dot, finally having discovered her whereabouts, with preternatural gravity.

"Say—little girl—say that 'gain, will you?" he said, slowly.

Dot quite innocently repeated it. The man carefully removed his hat and looked into it. Then he turned it over and shook it. Nothing, of course, fell to the ground.

"'Tisn't there. You fooled yourself. I thought so," muttered the man.

And then he leaned so far over that he dropped the hat in the gutter.

"You must be dreadful sick," Dot said to him, her little heart touched by his appearance.

"Yes—that's it. Sick. That's it," he mumbled.

This was a really awful adventure for little Dot Kenway.

"I'm going to get you a glass of water," she said. "Your face is so red. You are sick, I can see."

He said nothing, but blinked at her. Perhaps he did not at first quite understand. Dot turned to cross the street toward the store on the corner. Then she turned back.

"Will you please hold my Alice-doll while I go for the water?" she asked the man. "Do be very careful with her—please."

"Sure!" said the man, good-naturedly.

"You'll truly, truly be very careful of her?"

"Sure will," repeated the unfortunate.

So, after she had placed the doll carefully in his arms, the little girl tripped away on her errand of mercy. The man sat down on the curb and held it. It might have been a laughable situation—only no thinking person could have laughed.

The man nursed the doll as tenderly as Dot would have done herself. He rocked to and fro on the curb, hugging the battered doll and looking down at it earnestly.

Nobody had yet noticed the incident—save Sammy Pinkney; and Sammy Pinkney had run away.

Dot was bold in the cause of any one in need, if she was not bold for herself. She asked for the glass of cold water and obtained it. She brought it carefully back to the man on the curbstone, holding the glass in both her dimpled hands.

His face was still very red, but his eyes were no longer glassy. He looked at the child with a shamed expression slowly dawning in his countenance, and his eyes were moist with tears.

"You'd better take your doll, little girl, and get away from me," he said, but not roughly.

"Oh, no," said Dot, determinedly. "I must help you. I know you must be very sick. You ought to see our Dr. Forsyth. He could make you well quick, I know."

"I guess you can cure me as quickly as a doctor," said the man, hanging his head. "I—I had a little girl like you once."

"Now drink some of this," urged Dot, without noticing the man's last remark, and offering the glass of water.

He took it in a trembling hand and raised it to his lips. The little girl reached for the Alice-doll, but watched him carefully.

"Don't spill it," she said, "and don't drink it all. I think if I put some on your face you'd feel better."

Immediately she produced a diminutive handkerchief, folded just as it had been ironed, and when she took back the glass, she dipped the bit of muslin in the water remaining in it.

Then with tender hand she wiped his hot face; and she wiped away two big tears, too, that started down his cheeks. She was still engaged in thus playing the Good Samaritan when a swiftly moving motor car coming through Willow Street was suddenly brought to a stop beside them.

There was a thin, wiry fellow at the steering wheel. The goggles he wore half disguised him. In the tonneau sat a fat, prosperous looking man smoking a big, black cigar.

"That's him, ain't it, Joe?" asked the fat man, nodding toward the man sitting on the curbstone.

"Yep. That's him," rejoined the chauffeur.

"Hey, Mr. Maynard!" exclaimed the fat man. "Get up and get in here. I want to talk to you."

The fast sobering man looked up, saw the speaker, and did not look particularly pleased. He tried to rise. Although his brain was fast clearing, his limbs were still wabbly.

"Get out and boost him in here," said the fat man, in a low tone to the chauffeur.

The latter hopped out. He came quickly to the aid of Mr. Maynard, and pushed little Dot Kenway rudely aside. The man still held the doll.

"Say! you don't want that thing!" muttered the chauffeur, and he seized the doll and flung it disdainfully upon the ground.

Dot uttered a scream of terror. At that moment Agnes and Neale O'Neil, the latter carrying the girl's schoolbooks, came around the corner.

CHAPTER VI—THE BIG TOUR IS PLANNED

Mr. Maynard, as the fat man had called Dot's new acquaintance, grumbled something or other at the chauffeur because of his treatment of the Alice-doll; but he was not yet quite himself and the fellow merely laughed and urged Maynard toward the car. The fat man laughed, too.

"Come on, Mr. Maynard. We'll take you home," said the big man, holding open the door of the tonneau.

Just as Neale O'Neil and Agnes reached the spot, the chauffeur pushed Maynard in and stepped quickly into his own place.

"Say! what did you do to this little girl?" demanded Neale, with some heat, addressing the chauffeur.

The fellow did not answer; neither did the big man; and Maynard had tumbled into a seat without a word. Dot had already picked up her doll; it was not hurt. The car started and rolled away.

"The mean thing!" exclaimed Neale. "Don't cry, Dot."

"I—I'm not going to," sobbed the smallest Corner House girl. "I don't b'lieve they'll be kind to that man. He's awful sick."

"Who is?" asked Neale quickly, exchanging glances with Agnes.

"That man they took away. I got him a drink of water. But Sammy Pinkney told a story 'bout him."

"What did Sammy say?" asked Agnes, but her attention scarcely on what Dot was saying.

The little girl told her. "But he was sick. I know it. I got him a drink of water. He wasn't carrying a brick at all."

Neale had grinned faintly; but his face was quickly sober again.

"I know who that Mr. Maynard is," he said. "He used to work in the court house. I believe he was in Mr. Collinger's office—and he was a real nice man once."

"Why, he is now," cried Dot, listening with very sharp ears. "Only he is sick."

"Perhaps you are right, Dottie," agreed Neale, still gravely, but speaking to Agnes. "Anyhow, he lost his wife and then his little girl. He's gone all to pieces, they say. It's an awfully sad case. And do you know who that big man is?"

"No," said Agnes, still unnoticing and gazing after the disappearing car.

"That's Jim Brady. He's a ward leader on the other side of town. He's very powerful in politics——"

"Oh, Neale!" cried Agnes, suddenly, seizing her friend's arm.

"Hul-lo! What's the matter?" asked Neale.

"Do you know who that fellow was that drove the car? Did you see him?"

"No-o. I didn't notice him much. He had dust goggles on——"

"I know! I know!" cried the excited girl. "They concealed his face a good deal. But I saw the freckles."

"The freckles?" repeated Neale, wonderingly.

"Yes. Of course. It was that freckled fellow who spoke to Ruth that day."

"Not Joe Dawson?" cried the boy.

"Yes. If that's his real name. Oh, Neale! Let's have him arrested."

"Cricky!" ejaculated the surprised youth. "Arrest your aunt!"

Agnes burst out laughing at that—serious as she was. "Aunt Sarah Maltby certainly did not steal Mr. Collinger's motor car," she said.

"Well. We don't know that Saleratus Joe did," grinned Neale. "Come on home. Don't cry any more, Dot. Just the same I would like to punch that fellow who threw down your doll."

"Can't we find out who he is—all about him?" demanded Agnes.

"Maybe. That Mr. Maynard knows him, I s'pose. I could ask him. I used to clean Mr. Maynard's yard and sidewalks for him. I'll see," promised Neale O'Neil.

When the trio reached the Corner House that day, however, they found a subject afoot that put out of Neale's and Agnes' minds for the time being all thought of the stealing of Mr. Collinger's car. And yet the county surveyor's aunt had something to do with this very interesting topic under discussion.

Mrs. Heard was present, having a neighborly cup of tea with Mrs. MacCall, who was quite as much a friend of the family as she was housekeeper. Mr. Howbridge had chanced to drop in as well, and Ruth had arrived home ahead of the other Corner House girls.

"Oh, Aggie!" cried Ruth, running out of the sitting room where tea was being served, Uncle Rufus having rolled the service table in there at Mrs. MacCall's request. "Just guess!"

"Going to have rice waffles for supper," put in Neale, with a cheerful grin.

"That boy!" said the oldest girl, scornfully.

"What has happened?" demanded Agnes, excitedly. Ruth was seldom given to exuberance of speech or action, and she was plainly stirred up now.

"He says we can do it!"

"Huh?" grunted Neale, staring.

"Who says we can do what?" demanded Agnes, her blue eyes almost as wide as saucers. "How you talk, Ruth Kenway!"

"It will be most delightful, I am sure," said the older girl, more composedly. "We shall all enjoy it. And Mrs. Heard has agreed to act as chaperone, for Mrs. MacCall can't go, and you know how Aunt Sarah Maltby feels about the auto."

"Oh! I see," grumbled Neale. "A glimmer of intelligence reaches my brain. You are talking about the trip in the auto after school closes."

"Is that it?" cried Agnes, clasping her hands. "Oh, Ruthie!"

"That is it, my dear! Mr. Howbridge just spoke about it himself. He has known Mrs. Heard for years, you see, and he thinks she would be just the nicest person in the world to go with us."

"And so she is," agreed Agnes.

"Well," said Dot, who had listened in grave silence, "if we are going off on a long journey with our car, my Alice-doll must have her complexion 'tended to. You take her, Neale, and get her doctored," and she thrust the precious doll directly into the boy's hands, and marched out of the room with quivering lip. It was really very hard for the smallest Corner House girl to part from her most loved child even in such an emergency.

"There now! What did I tell you?" demanded Agnes, of Neale. "You've got your hands full."

"Of doll," he admitted, but he did not appear rueful. "I know just where they will fix her up as good as new," and he laughed. "I believe in preparedness. I foresaw this when I spoke about the doll the other day."

But now was the time to talk about the tour. Agnes had prepared for this since the very first day she knew they were to have the automobile. The height of her ambition was to travel in the most modern way—by motor car.

With Neale—and sometimes aided by her sisters—she had planned elaborate routes through the surrounding country—sometimes into neighboring states. She had borrowed maps and guide books galore and had purchased not a few. In fact, in a desultory way, she and Neale had picked up a smattering of knowledge of roads and towns and hotels and general geographical information which really might be of use if, as Ruth said they would, the Corner House girls should go on a tour in the new seven-passenger car.

They talked about it to the exclusion of almost everything else that evening, and Agnes spread the news abroad at school the next day. That the Corner House girls really owned a car was already an important fact to their school friends.

For Ruth and Agnes were not likely to be selfish in their enjoyment of their new possession. Stinginess was not a fault in the Kenway family.

On the very second Saturday after they had come into possession of the car Neale had taken out the older girls and a party of their friends in the morning, and in the afternoon Tess and Dot had played hostesses to a lot of little girls. As Mr. Howbridge remarked with a laugh, the cost of the new car was a mere drop in the bucket. Maintenance and gasoline were the items that would deplete the pocketbooks of his wards.

As for Neale O'Neil, he almost lived in the car.

Of course, the entire family had to try it—even to Linda. Linda enjoyed it, and in her broken English stated it as her opinion that "heafen could be not like dis." Which was a statement not to be contradicted.

Mrs. MacCall was doubtful about the utility of the machine after all. Uncle Rufus, when he went out with Neale and the little girls and not a few of the pets, including a couple of kittens and Tom Jonah, just clung to the seat-rail with both hands and actually turned gray about the corners of his mouth.

As for Aunt Sarah Maltby, she had set her face against the innovation from the first.

"But of course," she said, in her severe way, "it doesn't matter what I say or what my opinion may be. Nobody asks me to advise. I am a non-entity in this house."

That was the beginning. Ruth and Agnes and even Mrs. MacCall had to coax and plead and cajole before the old lady would promise to take a ride in the car. When she did, she dressed in her Sunday dress—the one she always went to church in—and carried her prayer-book.

This was a state of "preparedness" that amused Agnes and Neale very much. Aunt Sarah evidently expected the worst. She even carried in her pocket the peppermint lozenges which she always took to church with her and nibbled at in sermon time.

Indeed, Aunt Sarah, who was a pessimist at the best of times, approached the ordeal in such a way that Ruth really began to pity her.

"I don't care! she'd spoil all our fun," protested Agnes, exasperated.

But the older sister said: "Perhaps she can't help it after all, Aggie. And if she really is scared, I am sorry."

At that Agnes whispered sharply: "Look at her face!"

Neale was running the car carefully, but at a good speed, on one of the pleasantest and smoothest highways around Milton. The air was invigorating, the outlook was beautiful, and the car ran like a charm.

In a moment of forgetfulness, perhaps, Aunt Sarah's grim countenance had changed. It did actually seem as though there was a smile hovering about her lips. To the two girls who rode with her in the tonneau it seemed as though it must be impossible for anybody not to enjoy the ride.

"Isn't it splendid, Aunt Sarah?" queried Ruth, with shining eyes, leaning toward the old woman.

Instantly Aunt Sarah's face became—as usual—forbidding. She shook her head with determination.

"No, Niece Ruth, it is nothing of the kind," she declared. "I do not like it at all. I knew I shouldn't. I wish to return."

"Well!" Agnes had gasped in her sister's ear. "Don't try to tell me! If Aunt Sarah was not almost laughing then, why, then her face slipped!"

CHAPTER VII—WHAT SAMMY DID

School had closed, and the long and glorious vacation had been ushered in. The Corner House girls had now lived in Milton for two years, and felt very much at home.

They knew many people—Agnes said: "A whole raft of people," but Ruth did not approve of such language and accused her fly-away sister of learning it from Neale O'Neil.

"Poor Neale! Must he be blamed for all my sins?" asked Agnes, with a wry smile. She was mending a tear in a very good skirt—and she did not like to sew.

"Oh, I will not accuse him of being the cause of that, Aggie," said Ruth, pointing to the tear.

"You're wrong," retorted her sister with a sudden elfish smile. "If he had not chased me, to get those cherries I stole from him, I wouldn't have caught my skirt on the nail and 'tored' it, as Dot would say."

"Tomboy!" declared Ruth, rather scornfully.

"I don't care," Agnes said, biting off her thread. "I hope I'll never be starched and stiff."

"But you are getting older," went on Ruth.

"Not too decrepit to run yet," retorted Agnes, pertly.

Ruth laughed at that, and pinched her sister's rosy cheek. "Nevertheless," she said, "that is one of the skirts you will be obliged to wear on our tour."

"Oh! Our tour!" cried Agnes, ecstatically, clasping her hands. "Ouch!"

"What is the matter?" demanded Ruth, startled by her sister's squeal.

"Stuck my finger with this horrid needle," mumbled Agnes, sucking the pricked digit.

She went back to her sewing as Ruth went out of the room. In came Neale in cap, goggles, and leggings.

"Oh, Neale! Have you got the car out?"

"Why, Aggie!" cried the boy, without replying to her question, and eyeing the work in her lap askance. "I am surprised! You're just like Satan—as we had it in our lesson last Sunday—aren't you?"

"Well! I like your impudence. In what way, please?" demanded Agnes.

"Why, you're sewing tears, aren't you?" chuckled Neale. "And the Bible says the Evil One 'sowed tares.'"

"Oh, don't! It's too great a shock. But, are you going out with the car?"

"Been out," said the boy. "I took Mr. Howbridge over to Brenton Woods to catch the train for the West on the Q. V. We won't see him again until we're back from our tour."

"Oh, yes! Our tour!" repeated Agnes; but this time she did not clasp her hands in ecstasy. She looked at her pricked finger ruefully instead.

"And coming back," went on Neale, "I happened to run across Mr. Maynard."

"Oh, yes!" cried Agnes again, but in an entirely different tone.

"He'd been fishing. You see, he doesn't have much to do now that he's out of the surveyor's office. That's why he—he gets into trouble so much, I suppose. That and worrying about the death of his wife and baby. I brought him home in the car."

"Did you ask him about that Joe fellow?"

"Saleratus Joe?"

"Yes. If that's what you are bound to call him," Agnes said.

"I did. Mr. Maynard doesn't know the fellow personally. He didn't seem to remember much about that day he met Dot. He remembers her, though," Neale said, thoughtfully. "Asked about her in a shamefaced sort of way."

"I should think he would be ashamed."

"He is to be pitied," said the boy, soberly.

"Oh, yes. I suppose so. All such men are. But for little Dot to get mixed up with a drunken man——"

"It didn't hurt her," said Neale, stoutly. "And maybe it has helped him."

Agnes took a minute to digest this; and she made no further comment. But she asked:

"How about that Joe? Doesn't Mr. Maynard know anything about him?"

"He says not. Suppose we tell Mrs. Heard, and she'll tell Mr. Collinger. Joe Dawson has sometimes worked for Jim Brady, the big politician. Mr. Collinger must know if Brady is one of the men who have been trying to get those maps and the papers away from him."

"Well," said Agnes, "I hope we can help bring those auto thieves to book."

"Guess Mr. Collinger is more worried about his maps—if they got them."

"Oh, Neale! suppose they should steal our car? Wouldn't it be dreadful? We must catch them."

Neale laughed. "You're going to be a regular detective when you grow up, Aggie. I can see that," he said.

"Put up the hammer, little boy," advised Agnes. "Do you know that it has been decided when we are to start on our tour?"

"No. When?"

"Mrs. Heard telephoned that she will be ready to-morrow. We shall start some time the following day, so Ruthie just said."

"Good!" declared the boy. "Say, Aggie! we're bound to have a dandy time."

"Even if we weren't, I should be glad to get away from this place," said the girl, suddenly a little cross.

"Why?" asked Neale O'Neil, in surprise.

"Because of that pest, Sammy Pinkney."

"What about him?"

"He is fairly hounding us to death," said Agnes, with a sigh.

"What about?"

"He has begged to go with us every hour—almost—since he first heard we were going on a long trip in our auto." Then she suddenly giggled. "Oh, Neale! He has decided that it would be more fun to be an auto pirate than a salt water buccaneer of the old school."

"One great kid that," chuckled Neale, appreciatively.

"But he is an awful nuisance. He bothers the little girls whenever they go out of the house. He's told his mother he's going with us—and I suppose Mrs. Pinkney half believes we have invited him."

"Cricky!" chuckled Neale again. "I imagine she'd be glad to get rid of him for a few weeks."

"My, goodness, me!" exclaimed the startled Agnes. "She sha'n't get rid of him at our expense—no, sir! I won't hear of it. Neither will Ruth. And, besides, there isn't going to be breathing space in that car after we all pile in—with Tom Jonah and the baggage, too."

"I have an idea!" said Neale, wickedly, "that we ought to have an auto truck trailing us with all the furbelows and what-nots you girls will think it necessary to carry."

"Mr. Smarty!" Agnes scoffed. "Remember we went camping last summer and we know something about what to take with us and what not to take."

"That's all right," said Neale. "But the Corner House girls are not going to live under canvas this time—that is, not much. At the fancy hotels you'll all want to cut a dash. How are you going to do it?"

Agnes laughed at him. "Don't you suppose all that has been thought of?" she demanded. "Mrs. Heard will send a trunk, and so shall we, by express to the Polo House at Granthan. That is going to be our first 'fancy' hotel, as you call them. Then, when we leave there, the trunks will be shipped on to our next fashionable roosting place. But, oh, dear me! I don't care much about the hotels. I want to be moving," declared this very modern young American girl.

"Cricky!" grumbled Neale. "I bet if you have your way we'll get pinched for speeding in every county in the state."

Every waking hour thereafter, until, on the second day, the car was brought to the side gate of the Corner House premises, was a busy hour for the four

Kenways and Neale O'Neil. Mrs. Heard came over with her personal baggage, for the route the party was to follow would not take them anywhere near her home. Besides, it was better to pack the car carefully before the start was made, and thus find out where every piece of baggage—as well as every passenger—was to be placed.

The car was roomy and comfortable; but bags and suitcases of all descriptions—to say nothing of an excited Newfoundland dog—were bound to occupy much space.

Neale declared he had groomed the car "to the nines"—and it looked it. It was new enough, in any case, for everything about it to shine and glisten. A good mechanician from the public garage had been over it the day before and pronounced every part in perfect working order.

"But that doesn't mean that we can't get a blow-out before going a mile," growled Neale, who had worked so hard that he was rather pessimistic. "But, come on, girls, bring out the rest of the household furniture. You seem to have half the contents of the Corner House packed in already."

Ruth calmly ignored this, and went about final arrangements in her usual capable manner. Nothing would be forgotten, nothing overlooked when Ruth Kenway was in charge.

The little girls were just as busy in their way as their sisters. Tess and Dot were too much excited and far too much taken up with their own affairs, to pay any attention to Sammy Pinkney.

But that hopeful youngster stuck to Ruth and Agnes like a burr—and a very annoying one.

"Aw, say! let a feller go!" was his mildest way of pleading for space in the automobile for his own small self. "I won't get in your way."

"No," said Ruth, with the same decision she had expressed from the first. "No."

"Aw, Aggie! you know me! If you say I can, I can."

"You're the biggest bother in the world, Sammy Pinkney!" declared the second oldest Corner House girl.

"Won't bother you a mite. I'll help. I'll run errands——"

"What errands, I'd like to know?" scoffed Agnes.

"Well—you'll want somebody to run 'em when the car breaks down——"

That settled it! Agnes would not listen to him any further.

"Say! I'll give Dot my bicycle if you'll let me go," he urged on Ruth.

"I'd be afraid to have her ride it," laughed Ruth. "The only thing you ever did give the little girls, Sammy—that goat—has been a dreadful annoyance."

"Give us your bulldog, Sammy?" suggested Agnes, knowing that the very soul of the boy was knit to that ugly, bandy-legged beast.

"Ow!" groaned Sammy. He could not agree to that. "I tell you I'll do anything you want me to——"

"Stay at home, then, and don't bother us," said Ruth, somewhat tartly for her.

"Aw, do say I can go, Aggie," he pleaded for the last time with the other sister.

"I'd like to see you find room aboard that car!" cried Agnes, having finally packed the last bag and parcel in the tonneau.

At these words Sammy shot away like a rabbit and disappeared. Mrs. Heard and the little girls came out. Everybody else from the Corner House appeared to bid the party good-bye—even Aunt Sarah.

"It'll rain before you get far," prophesied this last person, grimly, "and you'll have to come back."

She would not admit that an automobile was fit to travel in during wet weather.

"What have you got in that basket?" demanded Agnes of Tess, suddenly pouncing upon the serious little girl.

"Oh, Aggie! Only two of Sandyface's grandchildren. You know, we haven't found names for them yet."

"Two kittens!" gasped Agnes. "What do you know about that, Ruth?"

"How about Billy Bumps, too?" said Neale, looking perfectly sober.

"Oh, he and Tom Jonah would fight," said Dot, proudly bearing her renovated Alice-doll in a brand new coat and hat. The Alice-doll really was a pleasure to look upon once more. Only, whereas her hair had originally been dark, now it was very blonde indeed, to match her pink cheeks and blue eyes.

"Of course, it isn't very respectaful," admitted the smallest Corner House girl, in speaking of the change in Alice's appearance. "But ladies do bleach their hair and make it blond; and Alice always did love to be fashionable."

Meanwhile Tess had been convinced by Ruth that an automobile tour was no place for two kittens. Tom Jonah was being taken along as a means of safety for the car. Agnes was quite sure herself that automobile thieves were only waiting their chance to steal this brand new motor car.

They all got into the car at last—Mrs. Heard, Ruth and the two smaller girls in the tonneau, heaped about with baggage, but comfortable. Tom Jonah crouched under Agnes' feet in front, where she sat beside Neale, his head sticking out of the car and his tongue displayed like a pink woolen necktie.

Everybody shouted "good-bye!" There were plenty of neighbors to call after the touring party. And those on the street, for the first few blocks, seemed to be greatly amazed and amused by the passage of the Corner House automobile.

"Goodness!" ejaculated Agnes, in some disgust, and trying to sit up primly, "what do you suppose is the matter with folks, anyway? One would think we were a circus parade."

"Humph! guess we do look funny," chuckled Neale. "I once saw a picture supposed to represent the good ship Mayflower as she must have appeared off Plymouth Rock, if all the antique furniture you hear about really was brought over by the Pilgrims, as people claim. They had to hang chairs and tables and highboys and lowboys and such things from her spars, besides having an awful deckload. And I reckon we look like a large family on moving day," finished the boy, with an expansive grin.

"We do not!" exclaimed Agnes, quite put out. "Look at that old gentleman stare. What's he saying—and shaking his cane, too?"

"Got me," returned her comrade on the front seat.

He increased the car's speed and they passed people too quickly for the latter to make themselves heard—if what some of them shouted was of importance.

The passing of the Corner House motor car seemed to interest and please the urchins along the way more than anybody else.

"Goodness!" murmured Mrs. Heard, "I never was so much stared at before, I do believe. What do you suppose is the matter with us?"

"They must all want to ride with us," said Tess, quite composedly.

"Well, they just can't!" cried Dot. "See that boy running and yelling, will you? Why, he can't catch up."

Once out of the city Neale (of course urgently pressed by Agnes) "let her out another notch," as he expressed it. The car ran as smoothly as though the road was macadamized—although few highways about Milton were so well made as that. But Neale was a careful and skillful driver already, and the springs of the car were excellent.

On and on the handsome car rushed, leaving little spirals of dust behind it, and sending the small fry of rural animal life scurrying out of its path. The peculiar interest shown by pedestrians as they passed through the town, was continued out in the country.

As Neale slowed down for a railroad crossing, taking it easily and carefully, although there was no train near and the gates were up, a boy yelled:

"Hi, there! Whip behind! Whip behind, mister!"

"Now! how foolish that is," gasped Agnes, as they jolted a little going over the rails. "What do you suppose that little imp meant?"

Neale only grunted. He was thinking, and although he increased the speed of the car a little, it was only for a short distance. Then he shut her down suddenly—and stopped.

"What's the matter?" demanded Agnes, curiously.

"Where are you going, Neale?" asked Ruth, as the boy crept out from behind the wheel, stepped over Agnes' feet and the dog, and leaped out into the road.

"I want to see something," muttered Neale. He went to the rear of the car. Then he uttered a shout:

"Come and look at this, will you? What do you suppose that kid has done?"

"What kid?" asked Agnes, following him nimbly out of the car. Tom Jonah bounded out, too, glad, probably, to stretch his cramped limbs.

"Sammy Pinkney!" said Neale, pushing back his dust mask and staring.

Ruth stood up to see over the folded-back top of the car. "What is it?" she demanded, unable to see anything.

But Agnes arrived beside Neale, and saw perfectly. "Well! I never!" she ejaculated. "Sammy Pinkney! how dared you? What are you doing here?"

For Sammy was roosting, more or less comfortably, on the back of the car, and had a bright, new russet leather suitcase tied on beside him with a bit of rope. He presented a grinning, dusty, befreckled face to Neale and the Corner House girl.

CHAPTER VIII—REFORMING A "PIRATE"

"Well! you said I could come, Aggie Kenway—so there!"

This was Sammy's initial statement when Neale dragged him off his perch and brought him around to the side of the car where all could see him.

"Why! you awful boy! I never!" declared Agnes, shaking her head at him angrily.

"Yes, you did," repeated Sammy.

"Don't add to your wickedness by telling such a story, Sammy Pinkney," admonished Ruth.

"Oh, Sammy!" gasped Tess, dolefully.

"I don't believe even pirates tell stories," added Dot, with grave conviction.

"I ain't! I ain't telling a story," repeated the small boy, with earnestness. "She did! she did!"

"I never! I never!" responded Agnes.

"Wait!" put in Ruth, firmly. "We are getting nowhere. Of course you did not tell him he could come, Aggie; but he must have thought you said something like that. What did she say, Sammy Pinkney?"

"She said—she said," choked the now much-abused-sounding Sammy. "She said she'd like to see me find room aboard the car—and I did!" and he concluded with something like triumph.

"Oh!" gasped Agnes.

"Well, I never!" exclaimed Mrs. Heard, and it must be confessed she was immensely amused. "What a boy!"

"Did you ever hear the like of that?" repeated Ruth, using one of Mrs. MacCall's favorite expressions of amazement.

"I'm sure I didn't mean——" began Agnes, but her older sister said, quickly:

"Of course you didn't, deary! And that boy should have known better."

"She did tell me so—she did!" wailed Sammy. "And I'm going. My mother said I could—and that you girls was awful nice to take me."

"Cricky!" murmured Neale, all of a broad grin now. "You got a reputation that time, Aggie, for goodness, without meaning it."

"I don't care——"

"The thing is now," interrupted Ruth, decidedly, "how to send him home."

At that Sammy lifted up his voice in a wail that might have touched a heart of stone. And really, after all, there was not a heart of stone in the whole party of tourists from the old Corner House—not even in Tom Jonah's breast. The old dog went up to Sammy and tried to lap his tears away.

"Oh, see here, kid! don't yell like that," begged Neale. "Turn off the sprinkler. That won't get you anywhere."

"Will you tell me what we are to do with him, then?" demanded Ruth, quite put out. "There is no room for him in the car."

"I can stay where I was. I don't mind," gulped Sammy.

"Never!" declared Agnes. "You made a show out of us all the way through town. We'll never hear the last of it."

"We were boarded by a pirate, sure enough," chuckled Neale.

"He's worse than any pirate," sighed Ruth. "We'd know what to do with a real pirate."

"I wonder?" murmured Neale, his eyes twinkling.

But Ruth ignored him. She thought she saw her duty, and was determined to do it. "I suppose we shall have to go back," she hesitated.

"Oh, no, Ruthie!" begged the two little girls in chorus.

"I wouldn't go back for that horrid little scamp!" snapped Agnes, her face flushing. "Sammy Pinkney, you are the worst boy!"

Sammy sniffed and looked at her. "I found that ring you lost that time, Aggie Kenway. 'Member?" he asked.

"But you are an awful nuisance," pronounced Ruth, with conviction.

"You never would have knowed your hens was layin' in Mr. Benjamin's lot last week if I hadn't ha' told you, Ruthie Kenway—so there," responded the youngster.

"And you told me that—that sick man was carrying a brick in his hat—and he wasn't," Dot put in faintly.

Sammy grinned at that; but he was prompt to say, too: "Well, who found all your dolls out on the grass where you'd played lawn party, and brought 'em in just before the thunder shower the other day? Heh?"

"Cricky!" exclaimed Neale, under his breath, and with some admiration, "the kid's making out a case."

Tess, the kind-hearted, would make no accusation; but Ruth, despite the boy's rejoinders, remained firm.

"No," she said. "He must go home. Is there a railroad station near from which we can send him, Neale? We'll telephone to his mother. We are a long way from town."

At that Sammy Pinkney, who prided himself on being "tough" and who was in training for a piratical future, broke down completely.

"Ow! ow! ow!" he howled, digging his grimy fist first into one eye and then into the other. "I don't wanter! I don't wanter! I don't wanter go back. I ain't got nobody to play with. And ma'll lick me 'cause I said you'd 'vited me to go—an' now Aggie s-s-says she didn't. And I been sick, anyway, and I can't play with the fellers, 'cause it tires me so.

"I—I—I never git to go nowheres," pursued Sammy, using the most atrocious English, but utterly abandoned in his grief. "You Corner House girls git all the go—go—good times, and I ain't got even a s-s-sister to play with——"

At this point a most astonishing thing overtook Agnes Kenway. She had begun by glaring at Sammy in anger; but as he went on to bewail his hard state, her pretty face flushed, then paled; her blue eyes filled with tears which soon began to spill over. She drew nearer to the miserable little chap, standing, dirty and forlorn, in the middle of the road.

"Now, stop that, Sammy!" she suddenly blurted out. "Just stop. Don't cry any more."

"He can't go. There isn't room," Ruth was repeating.

Agnes turned toward the eldest Corner House girl sharply and stamped her foot.

"He shall go, Ruth Kenway—so there! He can squeeze in on the seat between Neale and me. Here! take that bag up, Neale O'Neil. There's room for it right in here," and she pointed. "Now! stop your crying, Sammy. You shall go; but you'll have to be good."

"Oh, Aggie," cried the happy youngster, "I'll be as good as gold. You'll see."

"Well!" gasped Ruth, yet not sorry that for once Agnes had usurped authority.

Mrs. Heard laughed. Dot said:

"Well, it's true. He hasn't any sister."

"And I'm sure he can be good," put in Tess, the optimist.

Neale was chuckling to himself as he put Sammy's suitcase in the place indicated.

"What is the matter with you, Neale O'Neil?" demanded Agnes, hotly, brushing the tears out of her eyes.

"I was just thinking that this party has assumed a good deal of a contract," said the light-haired boy.

"What for?"

"For reforming a pirate," said Neale.

CHAPTER IX—A WAYSIDE BIVOUAC

Ruth insisted upon stopping at the first brook they came to and Sammy was made presentable—his face and hands scrubbed and his clothing brushed.

"Yuh needn't be so particular," said Sammy. "There'll more dirt get on me before night."

"Listen to him!" groaned Ruth.

Mrs. Heard laughed. "That's what it means to have a boy in the family. Oh, I know! I brought up my nephew, Philly, for the most part. I had to watch him like a cat at a mousehole to see that he did not go to bed at night without washing his feet. He would run barefoot."

"One of the penalties of going on this excursion, young man," said Agnes to Sammy, "is having to keep clean. I know it's going to be hard sledding for you; but we can't afford to have a grubby looking youngster in the party."

Sammy sighed, muttering: "Well! I guess I can stand it. Ma bathed me all over, every day, when I was sick. Guess that's why I'm so thin now. She purt' near washed me all away."

The first day's journey had been carefully laid out, and the party of tourists from the old Corner House knew just where they were to stay that night. They were not to be bound throughout their tour, however, by hard-and-fast plans or rules.

"It's a poor rule that can't be broken," said the matter-of-fact Mrs. Heard. "Just the same we want to know something about where we are going—sometimes. I wouldn't fancy being caught out in some wilderness on a stormy night, for instance, with nothing better than somebody's barn to take refuge in."

This, of course, neither she nor the others realized at the time was a prophetic statement.

Naturally, if one is to go on such an excursion as this of the Corner House girls, one must have some idea of the roads, of hotels, and of the choice of routes and hostelries, as well as distances between proposed stops.

As far as they had been able to learn there was no hotel on the road they had selected, near which they would be at noon of this first day. So, in with the suitcases and other impedimenta, was packed a lunch hamper.

When they stopped by a wayside spring for the noon bivouac, they were out of sight of every house and a long way from home. But Neale O'Neil knew this road.

"I was over it the other day with Mr. Howbridge. Pogue Lake is just back there a couple of miles. That's a great fishing place."

"I never did see how men and boys could be cruel enough to fish," said Mrs. Heard, with a little shudder. "Always wanting to kill something. Hooking fish by their poor, tender mouths—it's awful!"

"I should think it would hurt the worms worse than it would the fish, Mrs. Heard," said the thoughtful Tess. "The long worms get cut in half—and both ends wriggle so!"

"Huh!" grunted Sammy. "Worms ain't got no feelings. No more'n eels. And it don't hurt an eel to skin it—so there!"

"I'd like to know how you know so much, young man," said Mrs. Heard, tartly. "Did you ever talk to a skinned eel? Who told you it didn't hurt 'em?"

Other automobile parties had stopped at this pleasant spot to picnic, for there were unmistakable marks of its having been thus occupied. It seems seldom to occur to picnic parties that other excursionists may wish to use the same sylvan spot which they find so lovely and leave in such disgraceful condition.

But the party from the old Corner House was careful in more ways than one.

Strapped to the side of the automobile just over the step, was a folding tripod of light lacquered steel rods. From the apex of these when they were set up, the kettle was hung, for Mrs. Heard insisted she must have her tea.

First, however, Neale O'Neil produced a small shovel and prepared a patch of sand on the grass, on which to build the fire. He was an old hand at camping out and knew very well that fire could not spread from a sandpile.

Neale had always shown himself to be quick and handy; but Mrs. Heard was immensely pleased with his despatch in getting water boiled and his part of the camping arrangements complete. Of course, the girls "set the table," and even Sammy was made use of. He gathered the supply of dry fuel, and if Neale had not stopped him he would have piled up sufficient at the camp site for a Fourth of July bonfire.

It was after the older girls had washed the few dishes they had used and while they were resting after the lunch that the first incident of real moment on this tour of the Corner House girls occurred.

A man came tramping through the brush with a rod in his hand and a creel slung from his shoulder. He wore long wading boots and he walked through the brook into which the waters of the spring trickled, and so reached the automobile party. Tom Jonah stood up, but did not growl at him.

The man was lifting his cap and going right by when Dot Kenway uttered a squeal of surprise.

"Oh, Tess! Oh, Aggie!" she cried. "Here's my sick man now."

At the same moment Neale O'Neil recognized the fisherman and shouted to him:

"Hi, Mr. Maynard! What luck to-day?"

The other turned a single glance at Neale and nodded, his attention immediately becoming fixed on Dot. He approached her with a smile warming his countenance, which seemed rather saturnine in repose.

"This is my kind little friend," he said; and although his face was deeply flushed it was not from the same cause as when the smallest Corner House girl had previously met him. "So you remember me?"

"Oh, yes, sir," Dot replied, a little bashfully, giving him her hand.

"And how is the dolly's health? But this isn't the one?" asked Mr. Maynard, showing that he had a good memory for some incidents of that former unfortunate afternoon.

"Oh, yes; this is my Alice-doll," said Dot, eagerly.

"Why, she doesn't look the same," the man declared, warmly interested.

"She has new clothes on—and a new hat."

"I never would have known her again," went on Mr. Maynard.

"And you couldn't ever guess what's happened to her," said Dot, seriously.

"Her face——?"

"She's been completely cured of a dreadful bad complexion," confided Dot. "Neale took her to a hospital. It is wonderful what they can do to you nowadays at hospitals," said the little girl.

"It is indeed," agreed Mr. Maynard, taking the Alice-doll tenderly in his arms.

"I saw the place myself," went on Dot, eagerly. "There was a big gold sign over the door, 'Dolls' Hospital.' Why! I didn't know there were such places."

"Indeed?" responded the man, very much interested.

"Yes. And they fixed Alice's face—and her hair. Of course, she wasn't a real blonde before; but it's fashionable. Like our Aggie, you know," pursued the talkative Dot.

Meanwhile Agnes had been whispering eagerly to Neale and now they both approached Dot and her friend.

"Mr. Maynard," said Neale, "have you see anything of Saleratus Joe again?"

"My goodness, Neale!" exclaimed the fisherman. "You could have seen both him and Jim Brady on this road this very morning. They passed me as I came along to the pond, in that big car of Brady's."

Mrs. Heard had been attracted by this topic of conversation. She said:

"I believe that horrid Brady brought about the stealing of my nephew's car. And he's shielding the men who actually did it."

"I don't know about that, Mrs. Heard," said Mr. Maynard, who evidently knew the widow. "He surely didn't have the car stolen for his own use," and he smiled, "for that French machine of his cost him forty-five hundred dollars. He told me so the other day."

"Are you very well acquainted with Brady, Mr. Maynard?" queried the woman, rather suspiciously.

"Why—no!" he replied, slowly. "I know most of the men who hang about the court house; and Jim thinks he can get me back in the surveyor's office. Of course, I should be grateful if he could."

"I don't for a moment suppose that Brady wanted my nephew's car," said Mrs. Heard, sharply. "You know that?"

"Why—yes," responded the fisherman again.

"But if Brady had it stolen, why hasn't the car been found?" Neale put in, wonderingly.

"I told you before," said Mrs. Heard, promptly. "They expected to find those road maps. And I guess they didn't find 'em," she added, with a nod of satisfaction.

"You may be right, Mrs. Heard," agreed Mr. Maynard, but evidently desirous of saying no more.

He handed the Alice-doll back to Dot, who, with Tess, had not been much interested in this discussion, of course; and he picked up his fishing rod to depart.

"I am sorry I did not happen along before you ate your luncheon," he said, smiling. "I could have supplied you with a nice mess of yellow perch."

"Thank you, Mr. Maynard," said Agnes, with a naughty twinkle in her eye. "I'm afraid we should have had to refuse them, for Mrs. Heard does not approve of fishing."

"Goodness! but I am fond of fish, just the same," said their chaperone, honestly.

"What would you suggest as the least cruel way of capturing fish?" Mr. Maynard asked, soberly.

"How about seining them and then chloroforming each fish?" whispered Neale to Agnes.

But the widow laughed, saying to the fisherman:

"I remember my husband used to go fishing with you, Mr. Maynard. But he never brought fish into the house where I could see them till they were ready for the pan, so as not to shock me."

"That was quite right of him, Mrs. Heard," said Mr. Maynard, gravely. Then he turned to Dot again. "I hope you will all have a fine time on your tour—you, especially, my dear. Do—do you suppose you could spare a kiss for me—a good-bye kiss?"

"Oh, yes, sir," said the generous Dot. "And I truly hope you won't be sick again, Mr. Maynard."

The man flushed deeply, saying:

"I have not been troubled by that sickness, my dear, since the day you were so kind to me; and—please God!—I never shall be again."

He strode away then with a nod only to the others.

CHAPTER X—THE PASSING AUTOMOBILE

After the bustle of getting under way again had quieted down and the car was speeding merrily through the woodland and past the pleasant farms of the Oxbow Valley, Agnes began to talk eagerly to Neale O'Neil about the all-absorbing topic which occupied her mind.

"How much do you suppose Mr. Maynard really knows about the stealing of Mr. Collinger's car?" she demanded.

"Not a thing!" said her boy friend, promptly.

"Oh, Neale!"

"No. I know Mr. Maynard. He's a perfectly square man, I am sure. I don't suppose he ever noticed Saleratus Joe until I called his attention to him."

"Where do you suppose they have gone?" queried the girl, starting on another tack.

"Who?"

"That Joe and the Brady man."

"Ask me an easier one," laughed Neale O'Neil.

"But can't we do anything about it if we run across them?" she cried.

"Joe and Brady?" gasped Neale, in wonder.

"Yes."

Neale eyed her quizzically for a long half minute—that is, with one eye. The other he kept faithfully on the road ahead.

"Aggie," he said, "you beat the world. Mucilage isn't in it with you for sticking to a thing when your mind is once set upon it."

"Well, I don't care!" she pouted.

"Oh, yes you do. You evidently do care or you wouldn't be talking about that stolen car all the time. What's the odds where Mr. Brady and his chauffeur have gone? You don't suppose Brady knows anything about Mr. Collinger's machine himself, do you?"

"Of course he does! I believe he had it stolen," cried the girl.

"And if he did, so much the more reason for his not knowing anything about what was done with the car. That's what Mr. Maynard intimated. Brady would have no use for it. And I doubt if anybody could use it long without being arrested. Hard to hide an automobile nowadays. Unless the thieves took it away up into Canada and sold it, maybe."

"Surely that Saleratus Joe couldn't have done that," rejoined Agnes, instantly, "for he couldn't have gone there and got back so quickly."

"Good girl. Female detective, I tell you!" chortled Neale. "But how about the other fellow?"

"Who—that awful Brady?"

"Cricky! No. They say there were two fellows in Mr. Collinger's car when it was driven away from the court house. And maybe he—the second chap—has the car now."

"Oh, dear me! I'd like to know," sighed Agnes.

This first day's journey was rather long; the smaller girls were tired by mid-afternoon. So was Sammy Pinkney, although he would not admit the fact. Tess and Dot went frankly to sleep in the tonneau; Sammy kept himself awake by asking questions of Agnes and Neale, so that they could no longer discuss the stealing of Mr. Collinger's automobile, or any other subject of moment.

"If I ever go auto riding again with a kid of his size," growled Neale, at last, "I'll insist on having his question-asker extracted first."

"Huh! What's a 'question-asker,' Neale? Have I got one?" was the query that capped that climax.

The effort to reach a certain old-fashioned hotel on the road to Parmenter Lake, of which Mrs. Heard knew, was successful. Without even a minor mishap Neale brought the car to the Bristow House an hour before sunset and in plenty of time for supper.

As none of the four Corner House girls had ever slept in a hotel before, this was a new experience for them. Mrs. Heard engaged two double rooms for herself and the girls, and a third for Neale and Sammy. Tom Jonah was made comfortable in the stable yard.

The big dining-room was well filled when after they had washed, they went down to supper. The Bristow was popular despite the homely manner in which it was managed.

"Good home cooking," Mrs. Heard said, "and simple ways. These girls who wait on us are all from the neighboring families hereabout. It is not a popular resort with the sporty class of automobilists—although I notice that occasionally one of that kind gets in here."

Her remark was to the point, for at that very moment an example to prove the truth of it was furnished by a big man sitting alone at a small table at the end of the dining room.

"What?" he suddenly bellowed. "I can't get a drink here?"

"Tea, coffee, milk, or soft drinks," the waitress at that table recited, calmly. "The Bristow House is temperance."

The big man got up heavily, his face red, and refused to eat. "That settles it!" he growled. "I'd like to know what you keep a hotel for?"

"To feed people," said the waitress, wearily. She had evidently experienced a like incident before.

"That's Jim Brady!" whispered Agnes, in excitement, to Neale O'Neil.

Neale sat near a window. When the politician from Milton had stamped out, Neale peered around the window blind. The big French car was standing before the hotel.

"But say! that isn't the freckled-faced fellow with him," Agnes declared, peering around the other side of the window frame.

"No. New chauffeur. There they go—aiming for home. Guess he's left Saleratus Joe somewhere."

"I'd just like to know where," sighed Agnes, returning reluctantly to her supper.

By the time supper was over Sammy was again nodding like one of those mechanical figures shop-keepers sometimes put in their show windows to attract attention. Neale had almost to carry him up to the bedroom, and did have to help him undress after he was there.

"Cricky!" ejaculated the flaxen-haired youth, "I didn't start out on this tour with the expectation of nursing along a child, as well as an automobile. I'm going to have a lot of fun myself if I've got to play nursemaid for this kid."

Neale was really good-natured, however, and, for all his scolding, he helped Sammy off with his clothing gently enough. As Ruth had threatened, there was a bath made ready for Sammy, and that rite had to be administered before the sleepy little boy could creep between the sheets.

While Sammy was splashing in the bath a shout of laughter from Neale brought Mrs. Heard and the two older girls to the door of the boys' bedroom.

"What is the matter, Neale O'Neil?" demanded Ruth.

Neale was sitting cross-legged on the floor, rocking himself to and fro, and weak from laughter. "Look what the kid's brought with him in his bag!" gasped the older boy. "I was looking for his night clothes—and something clean for him to put on in the morning. See the mess of stuff I found, will you?"

It was a self-evident fact that Mrs. Pinkney, Sammy's mother, did not pack her little son's suitcase.

Neale had hauled out first of all a tangle of fishing tackle; a baking-powder box, well filled with a supply of squirmy fish-worms, kept moist in black soil that had sifted all over the contents of the bag through the holes in the cover of the box punched to give the worms air. There was Sammy's air-rifle in two sections and a plentiful supply of ammunition; a banana reduced to pulp; a bottle of matches; a sling-shot; a much-rusted bread-knife with its edge patiently ground upon a whetstone—evidently Sammy's idea of a hunting-knife or a bowie-knife.

In addition there was a very grubby-looking pocket-handkerchief in which were tightly tied two slimy garden snails; there was a piece of candy in a soiled paper, with a buffalo nickel imbedded in the confection; two brass wheels out of the works of a clock; last Sunday's lesson paper; two horse-chestnuts; and a pint flask with very suggestive looking contents.

"What?" gasped Mrs. Heard. "That boy carrying liquor?"

"And snails!" ejaculated Agnes.

"Such a mess!" exclaimed Ruth.

"But snails or the worms or anything else there," said the widow, severely, "will not steal away men's brains and make them ill. Where did that boy get whisky—or is it brandy?" she added.

Neale had finally extracted the cork. He first smelled and then tasted the suggestive looking liquor. Mrs. Heard gasped in horror. Agnes squealed. Ruth demanded:

"What is it?"

"It's what I thought!" said Neale. "Licorice water. Wonder the flask didn't break and drench everything with the stuff. And he has brought a few clothes."

"I see very plainly," Mrs. Heard said, when the laughter had subsided, "that the first town we come to of any size, we shall have to buy Sammy some needfuls. Goodness! how ashamed his mother will be when she learns of this."

Sammy was too sleepy to be questioned at that time about the wonderful contents of the suitcase; but in the morning he confessed that after his mother had packed the bag for him, he had been obliged to take out "a lot of useless duds" to make room for the necessary miscellany listed above which, to his boyish mind, was far more important.

However, it afforded the party a hearty laugh and Mrs. Heard (who declared her nephew—the now dignified county surveyor—had been just like Sammy) cheerfully purchased a proper outfit for the lad.

"I knew Sammy would be an awful nuisance," Ruth said.

"But, goodness! isn't he funny?" giggled Agnes.

The party made a good start from the Bristow House about nine o'clock. They were to run that day to Parmenter Lake, where they might spend some time, and to one of the hotels at that resort the trunks had been sent. They expected to have their lunch again in the open, and the hamper had been filled at the Bristow House.

Ever since the day the Corner House girls had first met Mrs. Heard and her brown pony, Jonas, there had been a matter puzzling Tess and Dot; and as time passed and the curiosity of their two active young minds was not satisfied, the children had grown more and more insistent in their demands on Neale O'Neil.

They wished to know what it was Neale had whispered into the fat brown pony's ears when the ex-circus lad had cured the stubborn creature's balkiness—for the time being, at least.

"I've always thought, Neale O'Neil, that you were better than most boys," Tess Kenway said, seriously, the subject having come up again on this morning's run.

"And he never was so stingy before," wailed Dot.

"If he'd only tell me what he said to Jonas," Tess went on, "we could say it to Billy Bumps when he balks. And you know he does balk sometimes—most awfully."

"Oh, Tess! maybe the same words that started the pony wouldn't start a goat. Would they, Neale?" asked the smallest Corner House girl.

But Neale only grinned, and refused to be drawn like a badger. The little girls could not get him to talk at all about the mystery.

And right here, while they were miles from any village—even while they were completely out of sight of any dwelling—a most astonishing thing happened.

Without previous warning the engine began to cough, and the car ran more slowly.

"Now what's happened, Neale?" inquired Mrs. Heard, rather nervously.

Neale made no reply at all for a minute. He tried first one lever and then another, ran slow, tried to speed up, and then found that in spite of everything he did, the engine was going dead.

He managed to get the automobile to the side of the road out of the way of other traffic before the engine entirely ceased to turn.

"Although there doesn't seem to be much traffic of any sort over this road," said Ruth. "We haven't been passed by an auto this morning."

"I should say not!" exclaimed Agnes, promptly. "Our car is no flivver, I'd have you know. Do you expect, Ruth Kenway, to have all the cars in Christendom pass us?"

"It looks now as though some of them might," responded the older girl, laughing at her sister's vehemence.

"I guess you've heard the story of the wealthy man who went out driving in his high-powered French car," remarked Neale, who had tipped back the hood and was looking to see if he could find what was wrong, "and his chauffeur drove too slowly to suit him.

"'This is like a funeral procession,' said the owner to the chauffeur; 'why don't you drive around that flivver in front of us?'

"'No use, boss,' the chauffeur told him.

"'Why not?' demanded the owner.

"'There'll be another flivver ahead of that.'"

"That's all right, Neale O'Neil," put in Agnes, smartly. "Trying to take our attention off the fact that we're not moving ahead very fast, either! What's the matter with it?"

"I—don't—know," confessed the boy.

He tried the starter and got a few feeble turns out of the engine.

"Nothing doing," he grunted.

"Is it something about the wiring?" murmured Agnes.

"Can it be the carburetor?" asked Ruth.

"Maybe something is out of gear underneath the car," suggested Mrs. Heard, briskly. "Don't they always have to get under the car to repair it?"

"Oh, yes!" groaned Neale. "'Get out and get under.' That's the auto-driver's motto." He pulled off his coat preparatory to doing exactly what Mrs. Heard had suggested.

Tess observed gravely:

"Well! this isn't something Neale can whisper to and make go when it balks."

To punctuate the laugh that followed this perfectly serious statement on the part of Tess, Agnes cried:

"Oh, listen! here comes another car."

The rumble of an approaching automobile was then heard by all, and it was coming over the same road they had come. Before it appeared around the nearest turn, they heard the warning "Honk! Honk!" of its horn.

There whisked into sight the next moment the rapidly-gliding automobile. Agnes was standing up to look back. Almost instantly she uttered another cry—this time almost a shriek:

"Oh, Neale!"

"Cricky!" was the boy's gasped rejoinder.

For as the strange car flashed by they had both recognized the man at the steering wheel as Joe Dawson; and the appearance of the fellow beside him was not a whit more confidence-breeding than was Joe's.

CHAPTER XI—AN ADVENTURE BEGINS

"That car was certainly not the stolen one," declared Neale O'Neil, after the automobile had whizzed out of sight in a cloud of dust.

"No; it wasn't a runabout," admitted Agnes. "But I just believe that man with Joe was the one who helped him steal Mr. Collinger's car."

"What are you two talking about?" demanded Ruth, for those in the tonneau had not recognized Saleratus Joe.

"Did you want to stop those men to see if they could help you, Neale?" asked Mrs. Heard. "It will be awful if we have to stand here all day. We're still a long way from Parmenter Lake."

Neale could not help uttering a grunt at that. Nervous people are very nagging—without meaning to be.

Just as he was getting down to crawl under the machine Sammy Pinkney, who had been keeping wonderfully quiet for him, suddenly asked:

"Say, Neale! You got any gas, do you s'pose?"

Neale straightened up, looked at the little chap who stood with his hands in his pockets and his legs very wide apart, and finally exclaimed:

"I don't know whether to be sore on you, Sammy, or not!"

"Huh? What's the matter?" asked Sammy, belligerently.

Neale O'Neil started for the tank. "Why didn't you suggest that before?" he demanded. "There! I declare, folks," he added, "the tank's almost dry. I should have bought gasoline before we left the hotel this morning."

"Goodness, gracious, me!" cried Agnes. "It can't be so, Neale!"

"It's empty," the boy assured her.

"And we stuck on this lonely road!" gasped Mrs. Heard. "No telling when another auto will come by."

"Oh, dear, Neale!" murmured Ruth, "how could you be so careless?"

"It's the easiest thing in the world to forget," the boy replied, with a quick grin.

"It was real smart of Sammy to remember about the gosoling, I think," said Dot.

"'Gasoline'—little goose," observed Tess, correcting her smaller sister, as she often did.

Agnes laughed outright. "Well, gosling is a little goose, sure enough, Dot." Then she added: "Now, Neale! what are you going to do?"

Neale O'Neil had opened the road guide and thumbed several of its pages.

"Last place we passed where gasoline is for sale, as I figure it, is twenty miles away."

"Oh!" was the chorused groan.

"But here!" added the boy, with sudden enthusiasm, "Procketts is but five miles ahead."

"What is Procketts?" demanded Agnes.

"Who is Procketts?" added Ruth.

"A village. Gasoline is sold there," declared Neale O'Neil, confidently.

"But five miles!" cried Mrs. Heard. "Will you have to walk there and bring back the gasoline yourself? That is too bad!"

Neale smiled more broadly and returned the book to his pocket.

"We'll run along to Procketts and get our fill of gas. It won't take long," he said.

"But, Neale!" Ruth began.

"How can we?" cried Agnes.

"Did you say the tank was empty, young man?" demanded Mrs. Heard.

"Not a drop in it," agreed the boy, answering the chaperone's question. "But— you see——" and he bent over and manipulated a small cock, "here's the emergency tank. That's always filled, you know; and it will run us to Procketts, all right."

"Well, you awful boy!" cried Agnes, half angrily. "You let us think we were stuck here."

"Cricky!" ejaculated Neale O'Neil. "Didn't you all just jump on me for being careless and thoughtless? And none of you thought of the emergency tank. A fellow's got to protect himself when he's alone with a parcel of females," and he chuckled.

"You ain't alone, Neale. I'm with you," declared Sammy Pinkney, suddenly.

The girls shouted with laughter; but Neale said, preserving his gravity:

"Thanks, old chap. I guess we menfolk will have to pull together in self-defence."

They came to the next village in the course of time, and Neale bought gasoline. Before one o'clock they reached a delightfully wooded place for camping, and proceeded to have lunch as they had made it the previous day. They all declared these rustic meals to be the best of all.

Just beyond the little grove was a pasture, and, looking between the bars of the old stake and rider fence, Tess and Dot saw that the open space was studded with flowers of several kinds.

"Let's pick some for Ruthie," Tess suggested.

"Let's. And for Mrs. Heard," agreed Dot.

She ran back for the Alice-doll—for of course that precious child had to pick flowers, too—and to tell the older girls what they purposed doing.

Mrs. Heard was taking a nap in the car, which stood in the shade by the roadside; the older girls were clearing up after the lunch. Neale and Sammy had gone in the opposite direction, across the road, where there was a pond and the promise of a bath, and Tom Jonah had gone with them.

So nobody gave the little girls much attention when they crept through the fence and out of sight of the camping place.

Tess and Dot did not intend to go far. There were plenty of flowers in sight of the place where they entered the pasture.

But you know how it is. The patches of blossoms at a distance appeared much more inviting than those close to the fence. The little girls ran from one to another patch, calling each other, delighted to find such a wealth of lovely, brilliant blossoms.

"I never did see such a lot of flowers in all my life, Dot Kenway!" cried Tess.

"Maybe this is the place where all the flowers started from," suggested the philosophical younger sister.

"Where all the flowers started from?" repeated Tess. "What do you mean, Dot Kenway?"

"Why, didn't the flowers have to start somewhere—like everything else? Our teacher says everything has had a beginning—like the first horses, and the first cow, and—and Adam and Eve, I s'pose."

"Humph!" said the less orthodox Tess, "who told you there had to be a first flower, anyway? Nonsense!"

"How did they come, then, if they didn't spread—oh! all around—from some place like this?" demanded Dot, quite excited.

"Oh, they just came," declared Tess. "I suppose," she added, reverently, "that God just thought flowers, and at once there were flowers—everywhere."

Dot stood up, picking up the Alice-doll, and holding all the blossoms she could carry in her other hand.

"Well," she said, softly, looking out across the field so spangled with the gay flowers, "He must have thought hard about 'em when He made this place, Tessie, for there's so many."

The next moment the smallest Corner House girl forgot all her unfledged philosophy, for she suddenly shrieked:

"Oh, Tess! Oh, Tess! Look at that awful, terrible bull!"

Tess was so startled by her sister's cry that she jumped up, scattering the blossoms she had herself gathered.

"Where? What bull?" she demanded, staring all around save in the right direction.

"There!" moaned Dot, who was dreadfully afraid of all bovine creatures, crushing both her flowers and her Alice-doll to her bosom.

Tess finally saw what Dot had beheld. A great head, with wide, dangerous looking horns, had appeared above a clump of bushes not far away. The animal was calmly chewing its cud; but the very sidewise motion of its jaws seemed threatening to the two smallest Corner House girls.

"Oh, Tess!" moaned Dot, again. "Will it eat us?"

"Bulls—bulls don't eat folks," stammered Tess. "They—they hook 'em. And how do you know it is a bull, Dot Kenway?"

"Hasn't it got horns?" gasped the smallest Corner House girl. "Of course it is a bull. Come, Tess Kenway! I'm going to run."

There seemed nothing else to do. Cow, or bull, it mattered not which—both were comparatively strange animals to the sisters. Most of the cattle they had seen were dehorned.

They now scampered away as fast as they could from the vicinity of the threatening peril. To add wings to their flight the creature lowed after them mournfully.

"Oh! I just know he wants to eat us," gasped Dot.

"Hook us, you mean," corrected Tess, strictly a purist even in her terror.

They scrambled on, panting. Tess tried to take Dot's hand; but the smaller girl would drop neither the doll nor the flowers. Finally they reached the fence at the edge of the woods, and plunged through it. Thus defended from the enemy (which had not followed them a step) the little girls fell to the ground, breathless, but relieved.

"That nawful, nawful bull!" groaned Dot. "I did think he'd get us before we reached the fence. See Alice! She's just as scared as she can be." And as the blue-eyed doll was a widely staring creature, Dot's statement seemed particularly apt.

"I lost all my flowers," mourned Tess.

"Well, there's a lot more yonder," said Dot, pointing ahead. "Mine aren't so good. I squashed 'em, running so."

"Well," Tess suggested, recovering somewhat from her fright, "let's pick some more. That old cow——"

"Bull!" interjected Dot, with confidence.

"Well, bull, then. He needn't think he's going to scare us so we can't carry a bouquet to Ruthie and Mrs. Heard."

"No-o," agreed Dot, rather doubtfully. "But I don't want to go back through that fence again, and into that field."

"We don't have to," declared Tess, promptly. She was standing up now and could see farther than Dot. "There's another open place where there're flowers—and there isn't any fence."

"And no bulls?" queried Dot.

"There can't be," Tess assured her. "They always fence up cattle. We shouldn't have gone through that fence in the first place."

So, having somewhat recovered from their panic, they pursued their adventure without for a moment considering that the farther they went in this direction, the greater the distance back to the place where their friends and the automobile remained.

Ruth and Agnes did not think anything about the absence of the two smaller girls until Neale, Sammy and the dog returned from their baths.

As Neale O'Neil came along from the pond and into sight of the automobile and the girls, he was laughing heartily, while Sammy's face was very red.

"What's the matter, Neale?" demanded Agnes, suspecting a joke.

"This kid'll be the death of me, girls," declared Neale, still chuckling. "I took along a piece of soap with the towels and told Sammy to see if he couldn't get some of the dust and grime off his face and hands. Cricky! I never knew a kid could get so much dirt on him between breakfast and noontime."

"Well, he looks clean now," said Ruth, kindly, seeing that Sammy was not very happy because of Neale's fun.

"I guess he is," Neale chuckled. "I said to him, 'Sammy, did you scrub your hands good?' And he said, 'Sure!' 'And wash your face?' 'Yep,' he answered.

And then I remembered the part of his anatomy that a kid usually forgets is hitched to him. 'How about your ears?' I asked him. And what do you s'pose he said?"

"I couldn't even guess," giggled Agnes. "What?"

"Why, Sammy said: 'I washed the one that's next to Aggie when I'm sitting in the car. You needn't tell her 'bout the other one,'" and Neale O'Neil burst into laughter again—as did all the others, save Sammy himself.

It was Sammy trying to turn the current of conversation from his ears, who discovered the continued absence of the two little girls.

"Where's Tess and Dot?" he inquired.

"Picking flowers," said Agnes, promptly.

"But, goodness!" added Ruth, "they have been picking them a long time. Ever since you boys went for your swim. They must have gathered a bushel."

"Go call 'em, Sammy," said Mrs. Heard. "We want to start now, I suppose. It's a long way to Parmenter Lake yet, isn't it?"

Neale pulled out the much-thumbed guide.

"Let's see," he said, fluttering the pages. "There's where we are—sixteen—no, seventeen miles beyond Procketts—where we bought the gasoline. That pond we just went to—Oh! that's Silver Lake. I bet it used to be called 'the mud-hole' before the day of automobile road guides.

"Just beyond, along this road, is what the guide-book calls 'a mountain tarn.' What's that, do you suppose?"

"A swamp," declared Ruth, promptly and wrongly.

"It's right near a village called Frog Hollow. Oh! 'Recently renamed Arbutusville.' What do you know about that?" chuckled Neale, delighted. "And a piece beyond there's a precipice, 'from the verge of which can be seen the ever-changing view of the entire eastern end of the Oxbow.' Cricky! I bet the view isn't half as changing as the names of these rural frog-ponds and the like. And I bet the precipice is a stone quarry," he added, with conviction.

"I expect that 'wayside inn' they speak of," said Agnes, who was looking over his shoulder, "is nothing but one of those squalid old beer-shops we see along the road."

"Humph!" commented Mrs. Heard, with a sniff, "it must take more imagination to get up one of those road guides for automobilists than it does to find all the virtues in a Presidential candidate."

Just then Sammy came plunging through the bushes. "Say!" he cried, "I can't find 'em."

"Why, Sammy!" said Agnes. "Why didn't you call Tess and Dot?"

"Did," he declared. "Been hollering my head off."

"Isn't that funny?" commented Agnes.

"I don't know whether it is funny or not," Mrs. Heard said, briskly. "Those children should be found."

"Yes. We're ready to start," said Neale.

"Surely they would not have gone far," Ruth added, in a worried tone.

Silence fell. The older members of the touring party looked at each other with growing apprehension.

CHAPTER XII—SEEKING

"Why, of course, the children are all right," Neale said, briskly. "Hold on! I'll make them hear."

He punched the lever of the horn several times and the clarion "Honk! Honk!" echoed through the grove.

"Oh, mercy!" ejaculated Mrs. Heard, with her hands over her ears. "That should wake the dead."

"Well, let's see if it wakes up Tess and Dot," laughed Neale O'Neil. "Come on, Aggie, let you and me run and find them."

"Don't get lost yourselves," Ruth called after them, laughing now.

After being startled for the moment by Sammy's report, all of them felt it was really impossible that Tess and Dot should be lost.

Neale and Agnes, with Tom Jonah in pursuit, ran over the slight rise out of sight, hand in hand and laughing, like the children they were themselves. They came to the fence and looked through it.

"Of course, that's where they are," Agnes said. "Do look at the flowers, Neale."

"They must have gone on down the hill," the boy agreed, and he and Agnes crept through the fence, on the trail of Tess and Dot.

They saw no trace of the children at first. And the mild-eyed cow that had caused all the trouble had disappeared. After a while Agnes cried out: "Oh, Neale! They picked flowers here. See the broken stalks!"

"Sure," he agreed. "Let's shout for them."

Again and again they shouted the little girls' names—singly and in unison.

"Where could they have gone—not to hear us?" demanded Agnes.

"Don't suppose they are playing 'possum, do you?"

"Oh, Neale—never!"

"But there's no place for them to go. You can see all over this pasture. Here, Tom Jonah! Find them! Find Tess and Dot!"

"We can't see behind all the clumps of bushes," suggested Agnes.

"But, cricky! are they asleep behind the bushes somewhere?" Neale demanded.

"No-o. Not likely," Agnes admitted.

"But—here!" shouted Neale. "What's this?"

He had found the place where Tess, frightened, as was Dot, by the cow, had stood up and dropped her great bunch of picked flowers. "What do you know about that?" the boy asked, quite seriously.

"Oh, Neale! Their flowers. They would never have thrown them away unless something had happened."

"But what?"

"I can't imagine," said Agnes, almost in tears.

"Neither can I," growled the boy, staring around the field. "Now, don't turn on the sprinkler, Aggie. Chirk up. Of course, nothing really bad has happened to them."

"Why hasn't there?" choked Agnes.

"Well, how could there? Right here almost in sight of the road. You girls would have heard them if they had cried out——"

"Do you think they've been carried off—stolen—kidnapped? Oh, Neale O'Neil! do you?" almost shrieked Agnes.

"Oh, stop it, you little goose—stop it," begged the boy. "Of course not."

"Goose yourself——"

"No; gander," said Neale O'Neil, determined now not to let Agnes see how serious he felt the disappearance of Tess and Dot was. "Now, Aggie, you stay here while I run around a bit and see what I can find."

He started off, Tom Jonah going too. The hot sun had almost immediately destroyed any scent the children may have left as they passed; and although the old dog understood very well what the matter was—that his two little mistresses had disappeared—he could find the trail no better than could Neale and Agnes.

Neale ran, shouting, toward the far end of the pasture. Almost at once he and the barking dog started something.

With a puffing snort, and a great crackling of brush, up rose the peaceful cow that had so startled Tess and Dot Kenway.

"Oh, Neale! come back!" shrieked Agnes, as she saw the wondering cow looking over the bush at her.

"What's the matter?" the boy demanded, while Tom Jonah approached the cow curiously.

"The cow!"

"Oh, she won't hurt you," declared Neale O'Neil.

"Just the same I'm afraid of her," said Agnes. "See her now!"

The cow was shaking her horns at the dog, and threatening him.

"Like enough she has a calf hidden away there in the brush," said Neale. "And——Cricky!" suddenly he added; "I bet she scared the kids."

"Oh, Neale!"

"Sure! That's what's the matter. They saw her and ran. And they ran in the wrong direction, of course," Neale continued, with very good judgment.

"Do you really think so, Neale?"

"Just as likely as not. Come here, Tom Jonah! She'll hook you yet."

"Oh!" said Agnes, quickly, "then we should be able to find the poor little things easily."

"Huh? How do you make that out?" Neale demanded.

"Why, if they ran in the wrong direction, we ought to follow them."

"That's all right," returned the boy. "But there are so many wrong directions! Which did they take?"

Agnes began to sob. Neale could not comfort her. Tom Jonah came and lapped her hands with his soft tongue, to show that he, too, sympathized with her.

The boy shouted until he was hoarse; but no childish cry was returned to him on the soft breeze.

And there was very good reason for that. The two smallest Corner House girls had some time since wandered beyond the sound of Neale's voice or the dog's bark,—even beyond the sound of the automobile horn.

While the older folk were seeking Tess and Dot, the two young explorers were seeking their friends. At first one could not have convinced the children that they were lost. No, indeed! It was Ruth and Agnes and Neale and Tom Jonah and Mrs. Heard and Sammy—and even the automobile—that had lost themselves.

"I don't see where they could have gone to," complained Dot, tired at last of carrying both the Alice-doll and her flowers so far.

"I didn't s'pose we'd come so far from that road," agreed Tess.

"Oh, I see it!" Dot cried, suddenly.

"The auto?"

"No, no! The road."

"Oh," said Tess, gladly. "Then we'll find them now."

The little girls climbed down a bank into a road which—had they known it—would have taken them out into the more important highway the motorcar was on. But unfortunately Tess and Dot turned in the wrong direction. They kept on walking away from their friends.

Had they not done this, or had they sat down and waited, Neale O'Neil and Tom Jonah would have found them in time; for they searched the patch of woods clear to this back road before returning, hopelessly, to the automobile to report their failure.

However, Tess and Dot walked and walked, until they really could walk no farther without resting. And then, having been absent from their friends for fully three hours, they had to sit down.

Dot cried a bit and Tess put her arms about her and tried to comfort the smallest Corner House girl. They had both long since thrown their flowers away, for the blossoms had wilted.

"Never mind, Dot," Tess said, trying to be very brave, "Ruthie and Aggie and the rest can't be far away."

"But why did they go off and leave us behind?" wailed the little girl. "And—and—I ache!"

"Where do you ache, dear?" asked the sympathetic Tess.

"In—in that funny bone that goes up and down my back," sobbed Dot.

"Funny-bone! Why, Dot!" cried Tess, "that isn't in your back. Your funny-bone is in your elbow."

"I guess I know where I hurt, Tess Kenway!" responded Dot, indignantly. "And it isn't in my elbow. It's that long, straight bone in my back I'm talking about. You know, Tess—your head sits on one end of it and you sit on the other. And it's all—just—one—big—ache——So there!" and she cried again.

"Now, I tell you what, Dot Kenway," said Tess, briskly. "There's one thing never does any good—not when your folks is lost from you."

"Wha—what's that?" choked the smallest Corner House girl.

"Crying," the older sister said, firmly.

"We—ell," sniffed Dot.

"So let's not do it. We can rest here as long as you want. When your backbone stops aching, we can go on."

"But where'll we go to?" was Dot's very pertinent query.

"Why—why, we'll just walk on—along the road."

"And where does it go to?"

"Why, does that matter?" returned Tess, bravely. "Of course our automobile will come along and pick us up. Or, if it doesn't, we'll reach a house and the lady will invite us in."

"Well," whimpered Dot, "I don't care how soon we reach that house—and the lady 'vites us in—and gives us our supper. I'm hungry, Tess."

"Don't you s'pose I am, too?" asked the older girl, with some asperity. Dot did sound rather selfish. "And Alice?"

"Oh! the poor, dear child must be just starved," sniffed Dot, hugging the doll closer.

"But she isn't complaining all the time," said Tess, scornfully.

Dot fought back her tears. "I think you're horrid, cruel, cross, Tess Kenway!" she said. "But I'll try not to cry."

There was reason for the children's hunger. It was now after six o'clock, the sun had disappeared behind the woods, and they had walked a long way.

Once they heard a great crashing in the bushes.

"Bears! bears!" whispered the excitable Dot.

"No-o," Tess said, gravely. "It didn't say anything about there being bears in this neighborhood, in that book of Neale's. If there were bears, he'd have told us about them."

"Well—well——whales, maybe."

"Goodness, Dot! you are the tryingest child! Whales live in the sea."

"Don't they ever come out?"

"Of course not," declared Tess, with conviction.

"Not even to rest themselves?" demanded Dot, with wonder. "I should think they would get awful tired swimming all the time. It must be more tireful than walking," and she sighed.

"Tire-some," corrected Tess, but without enthusiasm, and thinking of the whales. "Perhaps they come into shallow water and lie down on the bottom of the sea with their heads sticking out to breathe. Yes, that must be it."

"Oh, dear!" sighed Dot, for at least the twentieth time, and with lapsing interest in the whale. "Oh, dear! I wish Tom Jonah were with us."

"So do I! So do I!" agreed Tess, for as dusk came on she, like the smallest Corner House girl, was becoming truly frightened.

The disturbance in the bushes was repeated, and the children tried to run. A loud bell jangled—a most annoying bell; and in the distance a voice sounded:

"So, boss! So, boss! So, boss!"

It only frightened Tess and Dot the more to hear such strange sounds. They had never before heard the cows called home. And, besides, after their recent experience, they would have been only the more disturbed had they been aware that the thrashing in the bushes was Sukey, getting ready to go up to the bars to be milked.

No house did they see, however; not even a barn. They were on a back road, very seldom traveled, and the farms, what few there were in the neighborhood, faced on other highways.

The children trudged on, hand in hand, both crying now. Tess was weeping softly; but Dot was crying aloud, not caring who heard her.

When they came to a field beside the road, Tess stared all about for a light. But there was no beckoning lamp in a farmhouse window; nor even a flickering lantern to point the way to the farm outbuildings.

The streak of violet, shading to light blue, that evening had painted along the horizon with her careless brush, disappeared. Tall, black figures of trees upreared themselves between the children and the sky, and seemed to stalk nearer, threateningly.

A great nightbird floated out of the wood and swept low across the field with a "swish, swish, swish" of powerful wings. When it rose into the trees again it said:

"Who? Who-o? Who-o-o?"

"Oh! Who is he?" gasped Dot, clinging close to her sister.

"Mr. Owl," said Tess, promptly. "You know you've heard about owls, Dot Kenway!"

"But—but I didn't know they could talk," breathed the smallest Corner House girl, with a sigh. "Tessie, I can't walk any farther," she suddenly announced. "It isn't only that funny bone in my back; but my ankles are breaking right off—so now!"

"But—but there isn't any good place for us to stop till our automobile comes along," hesitated Tess.

"I don't care, Tess Kenway! I've got to stop!"

That settled it. At the edge of the dark wood the two little girls crept up on a grassy bank, between two roots of a great tree, sheltered at the back by a thick brush clump, and there they sat, clinging to each other's hand.

They were too frightened to talk. Too alarmed even to weep any more.

Around them, when they were still, scurried the little creatures of the night—the field mice, and the moles, perhaps, and the baby rabbits, and other small animals who shiver—as Dot did—when the great owl swoops low, crying his eternal question:

"Who? Who-o? Who-o-o shall I take for supper?"

The small fry of the fields and woods tremble at that cry more than did the two lost Corner House girls.

There may have been other enemies of the helpless, furry little animals lurking near, too—the weasel, the polecat, the ferret; even a red fox might have wandered that way and joined the bright-eyed company that kept watch and ward over two sleepy, sobbing children.

But nothing harmful was near them and, finally, Tess and Dot Kenway slept as sweetly and as soundly as though they were in their own beds in the old Corner House in Milton.

CHAPTER XIII—THE GREEN AND ORANGE PETTICOAT

Ruth and Agnes Kenway were in tears. Once before—when the Corner House girls were at Pleasant Cove—the two smaller sisters had been lost, and on that occasion circumstances seemed to blame Agnes.

Now neither of the older girls was to blame for the absence of Tess and Dot. Mrs. Heard said so. But both Ruth and Agnes felt condemned.

After searching the pasture and the patch of woodland beyond it, clear to the back road, Neale, disappointed, was inclined to scold Tom Jonah for not picking up the trail of the lost children.

Tom Jonah, however, was not a hunting dog; his nose was not as keen as some breeds possess—especially now that he was old. But he showed almost as much anxiety as his human friends on this occasion.

"Don't scold him, Neale," begged Agnes, sobbing. "He'd find Tess and Dot if he could—poor old fellow. See! he knows what I am saying."

The dog whined and lay down, panting. Indeed, it did seem as though there was nothing more to do here. The children, whether they had wandered away or had been carried off, certainly were not in the vicinity.

"Two hours have been wasted," said Mrs. Heard; "although we did not know we were wasting them, of course. We had to do what we could toward finding the children near by. But now we must waste no more hours. We must get help."

"Oh! what help?" cried Agnes.

"We must run to the next town—Frog Hollow," said Neale, in an undertone"—and get the constable or sheriff or somebody. We must start a crowd with lanterns to beat the woods. Maybe somebody has seen the children. They may be safe already in somebody's house."

"Or in the police station," put in Sammy Pinkney. "I got lost once and that's where they found me. Of course, I was a kid then. The cops was real good to me. One of 'em bought me ten cents worth of butter-scotch—you know, that awful, sticky, pully candy, Neale. And when my father come I couldn't holler to him 'cause my teeth was all stuck up."

"I bet that cop gave you the candy on purpose to shut your mouth," growled Neale. "You were talking them to death, it is probable."

"Oh, dear, me!" cried Agnes, "don't let us just talk; let's do something."

"Mrs. Heard is quite right, I can see," Ruth observed, recovered now in a measure from her first panic. "We must ask the authorities to help us. I should have been more careful."

"Why, Ruth," said the chaperone, "don't blame yourself. How could you have foreseen this?"

"I should not have allowed them out of my sight without Tom Jonah with them," the oldest Corner House girl declared. "Nor will I again on this trip, you may be sure."

"Come on, now," growled Neale, who felt very much disturbed about the loss of the little girls but who, boy like, did not wish to show his feelings. "Come on, now; we've talked enough. Let's do something. Get in here, Tom Jonah—you useless old thing! You're not half a dog or you'd have been able to follow 'em."

The big Newfoundland, with drooping flag and sheepish look, scrambled into the front of the car. So did Sammy. The automobile started and they sped away toward Frog Hollow, or Arbutusville, each revolution of the wheels taking them farther and farther from the lost children, sleeping under the great tree at the edge of the distant wood lot.

The automobile party were to spend a very anxious night—much more so than Tess and Dot Kenway, who had sobbed themselves to sleep among the huge tree-roots. Their sylvan couch was soft; the night was warm; and not a thing disturbed them after their eyes were shut.

A fretful bird, crying in the dusk of early dawn, aroused Dot for a moment; but she found Tess beside her, so went off to sleep again without realizing that she was not in her own bed at home.

Dawn soon smeared her pink finger-prints along the gray horizon. Other birds sleepily awoke. The morning breeze rustled the leaves, which took up their eternal gossip again just where it had ceased when the night wind died.

One morning call after another resounded through the forest patch. The light grew stronger and the tiny, furry things crept away to bed. The owl had long since ceased his querulous call. A feathered martinet that had at intervals, all the night long, declared for the castigation of "poor Will," pitched for a last time upon a dead limb at the edge of the wood and shouted forty-three times in succession: "Whip-poor-will!" without awakening Tess and Dot Kenway.

They slept on as day broke and the World yawned and threw off the coverlet of night to hop out of bed. The first red ray of the sun finally slanted over the tree-tops and struck right into the face and eyes of the smallest Corner House girl.

"Oh, my! I don't like that sun," complained Dot. "Mo—move over, Tess Kenway."

Tess' eyes popped open and she was immediately wide awake, while Dot was still snuggling down and trying to go to sleep again.

"Well, Dot Kenway!" exclaimed the older girl, "do you know what we've done?"

"No-o," mumbled Dot.

"Why! we've slept all through the night."

"Aw—ri'," Dot said, with very little interest.

"And do you know where we are?" pursued the lively Tess.

"I—I——Oh! is it time to get up?" yawned Dot.

Then she opened her eyes, too, and saw what Tess saw—the curve of the shaded road stretching away into the wood. The two little girls had been well sheltered under the thick umbrella of the tree; but in the open the grass blades sparkled with dew.

Birds hopped about, hunting their breakfasts—big, fat robins in their red vests; a chattering jay that flirted his topknot knowingly as he peered at the two Corner House girls; a clape, running spirals around a neighboring tree trunk like a little striped mouse, and looking at the children with interest. Across a broken wall a red squirrel ran—that pirate of his tribe. A rabbit started suddenly from his form in the grass, and, with a resounding thump or two, shot off across the field as though hearing a sudden call to breakfast at his house. The stirring of the little girls stirred everything else here to sudden activity.

"Why, dear me, Tess Kenway," gasped Dot, "we—we didn't get home, did we?"

"I guess we didn't," cried Tess, getting up quickly.

"Oh! nor we didn't find the automobile," added Dot, the memory of what had happened returning quickly. "Why, Tess! we're lost."

"Well, I guess we are," admitted her sister. "I thought Ruth and Agnes and the others were lost; but I guess it's us, after all, who don't know where we are."

"Wha—what'll we do?" asked Dot, yawning again, and scarcely alert enough yet to appreciate the serious side of the situation.

"Well! we needn't be afraid of anything now that it's daylight. Come along, Dot—let's find a brook," said the practical Tess. "I want to wash my face."

"We haven't any towels," objected Dot, trotting along the road beside her sister. "Nor any soap, Tess."

"Why! what do you suppose the squirrels and the rabbits and all the other woodsy things do for towels and soap?" demanded Tess, briskly. "I guess water's clean; it'll wash you."

"And our teeth-brushes, Tess?"

Tess overcame even that seemingly insurmountable difficulty. After they had found the brook—a quiet brown pool beside the road—and had bathed their faces and hands, Tess broke a twig and chewed the end to a brush-like swab, and so brushed her teeth thoroughly. Dot followed her example, and laughed.

"We are two wild girls," she declared. "We haven't any home—nor anything. That is, for a little while," she added, rather doubtful as to how this new game would "pan out."

"Why, when our clothes wear out we'll have to make new ones. And for Alice, too."

"How?" asked Tess, in turn curious. "What out of?"

"Oh, we'll weave new dresses out of grass and leaves, and trim them with flowers," declared the smallest girl, gaily.

"Well, so we could," agreed Tess, catching fire from her sister's enthusiasm.

"Of course. And shoes——"

"Oh, I know!" Tess cried. "We'd find rushes beside the pond and weave basket-work sandals to wear 'stead of shoes. And we might weave hats—like the Chinese do. And we'd build ourselves a house, and thatch it all over to keep the rain out—"

Dot had suddenly grown silent and allowed Tess to do all the talking. Tess looked at the smallest Corner House girl quickly. Dot's lips were puckered into a pout and her dark eyes were filling rapidly.

"What is the matter now, dear?" Tess asked, tenderly.

"Do—don't let's talk about it any more," choked Dot. "Besides, I'm hungry."

Tragedy stalked into the situation right then and there. They had no more imagination to waste upon the supposed life of a "wild girl." The principal question was: How were two little girls, fast becoming "wild," to eat?

They were walking along the road again when Tess suddenly spied something which brought a cry of delight from her lips.

"Look! Look, Dot!" she said. "What's on those bushes?"

The bushes in question overhung the bank above their heads.

"Oh, Dot! aren't those blueberries?" the older girl added.

"Of course they are, Tess Kenway," agreed her sister. "My, I could eat just bushels of 'em."

They scrambled up the bank and climbed the wall. Not only was there this clump of berry bushes which they had first sighted; but back of the wall was a great field, rocky and barren otherwise, but a fine berry pasture.

Farther out where the sun shone, the berries were larger and more had ripened. The little girls went on and on, picking the berries in handfuls and actually cramming them into their mouths. They were very hungry.

Their fingers and lips became stained; and if the truth were told some of the crushed berries left stains upon their mussed frocks as well as upon their faces. They reached the farther end of the field before they realized that they were so far from the road.

Tess was about to suggest that they go back. Somebody might come by on the lonely road they had been following. And then she saw the orange and green petticoat fluttering in the bushes.

"Oh, Dot! what's that, do you suppose?" Tess whispered, seizing her sister quickly by the hand.

"Oh-ee! A bear?" returned Dot, without even seeing the gay garment beyond the brush clump.

"Goodness! A bear that color?" demanded Tess, with some exasperation.

Suddenly the wearer of the gay garment stood up. She was a very brown woman, with great hoops of gold in her ears, and she wore other gay garments besides the green and orange petticoat.

"Oh!" murmured Tess, again, "I—I believe she must be a Gypsy woman, Dot Kenway."

Had the two little Corner House girls not been so much excited at just this minute they must have heard the passing of an automobile on the road, now out of their sight. Or, if Neale O'Neil had chanced to blow the horn just then Tess and Dot would surely have been attracted by the sound.

To the older Corner House girls and to Mrs. Heard that night had certainly been one of extreme anxiety. Neale had found lodgings for them in the squalid little village which the post-office authorities recognized as "Arbutusville," but which was still "Frog Holler" in the minds of the older inhabitants.

Neale found, too, a number of kind-hearted persons who were easily interested in the fate of Tess and Dot Kenway. There was a constable, and with that official at their head a dozen men started abroad at nine o'clock, with lanterns and a pack of "'coon dogs," to beat up the woods all about the place where the automobilists had camped.

Neale went with them; but despite Agnes' determination to attend she was refused the privilege. And Sammy, of course, remained with the women—they needing the protection of some manly spirit—and fell asleep in two minutes.

Neale O'Neil dragged back about dawn. The search had been resultless—save that the dogs had started a raccoon—and the party had swept woods, fields, and swamps for miles as well as it could be done at night. They had shouted.

They had roused every householder. Nobody had heard of the lost children or seen them.

But Neale had heard one thing that greatly troubled him; and yet which offered a possible clue to the little girls' disappearance.

On the way back to the village somebody in the crowd of searchers had told him that one of the aroused householders had mentioned the fact that there was a Gypsy encampment not many miles away.

The boy was instantly excited. He learned from his informant just where the camp was, and immediately put the idea before the constable.

"Why, that's too fur away, bub," said Constable Munro. "It's five mile beyond where you an' your folks stopped to eat—and on another road."

"The children might not have walked all that way," said Neale O'Neil. "They might have been carried there."

"Uh-huh? Against their will?"

"Well, why not?" returned Neale. "We hear all kind of stories about Gypsies. I've seen some bad ones myself."

"Aw, they're petty thieves, and bad horse traders sometimes. But to steal a couple of kids—I dunno 'bout that. Still—if you air bound to go there——"

"I am," Neale declared. "I'll have the machine ready as soon as I get a bite of breakfast."

He was sorry to have no good report to make to the girls and Mrs. Heard, and could only tell them, while he ate his hasty breakfast, where he was going and what he hoped to accomplish.

"I'm going with you," announced Agnes and Sammy in a breath.

"No," he said to the girl. "You can't go. The constable won't like it."

"Well, I don't see——"

"I am sure you would not like to go with a party of rough men," said Mrs. Heard, with such finality that Agnes became quiet.

But that did not stop Sammy's teasing. "Say, us men ought to go, anyway," he said. "Come on! Lemme go, Neale. I won't be in the way. Tom Jonah's going."

So in the car that had passed so near the two little lost girls as they picked berries, were Neale and Sammy, as well as Tom Jonah and the constable, Mr. Munro. Tess and Dot were too greatly interested just then, however, in that vivid petticoat and in the strange looking woman who wore it to think about anything else.

CHAPTER XIV—WITH THE ROMANY FOLK

The woman had a very brown face and wore great hoops of gold in her ears, while on her head was a sort of turban with a fringed end hanging down behind. She certainly was dressed in very gay colors.

She had bright, beady black eyes, and when she saw Tess and Dot Kenway she looked at them very kindly indeed. At least, her smile was broad and her voice, when she spoke, was pleasant. She carried a heaping basket of berries.

"You leetle children out early to pick the berry, eh?" she asked.

"Yes, ma'am," said Tess, gravely.

But Dot was more communicative. She said promptly: "We've been out all night."

"Picking berries?" queried the woman. "Not alone, eh?"

"We only just found the berries," declared Dot, the chatterbox. "And, oh! we were so hungry."

"You are out all night?" asked the puzzled woman. "Is it so?"

"We—we got lost from our folks," Tess said, at last.

"You leeve near here, eh?"

"Oh, no," said Tess, now more communicative, "We live in Milton. We were riding in an automobile——"

"No, we weren't!" interposed Dot, rather impolite in her eagerness to get the story perfectly straight. "We were stopping for lunch. Right beside the road. And Tess and I came to pick flowers."

"So you wandered from your friends?" asked the Gypsy. "I see. I see."

"And," added Dot, confidently, "we're hungry."

"Oh, Dot!" exclaimed the scandalized Tess. "Not now! Not after eating all these berries!"

"Huh! what's berries?" demanded the smallest Corner House girl. "I want an egg—and milk—and hot muffins—and——"

The Gypsy woman laughed merrily. Although she did not speak English quite like other people, she seemed to understand the language well enough.

"You leetle 'Merican girls come wit' me," she said. "I will find you food. Then we will find your friends."

Tess was a little doubtful of their new acquaintance. She had some fear of Gypsies as a tribe. This one seemed kind enough, and looked kind enough. Nevertheless, Tess felt that they should be careful while in her company.

But she could not explain this to Dot, and Dot was a prattler. The smaller girl's tongue went as fast as a mill-clapper, as Aunt Sarah Maltby often said; and it was particularly energetic this morning as she trotted along beside the Gypsy woman in the green and orange petticoat.

"Ah," said the woman, at last, "your people are reech, eh? They have one of these motor cars, and you leeve in a fine, big house? They will give reward, then, to get you back, eh?"

Just then, before either Tess or Dot could make a rejoinder, they broke through the bushes and entered a beautiful little park in which was pitched the Gypsy camp.

Of course, the two smallest Corner House girls had often heard of Gypsies. Indeed, they had seen more than a few of them. The women often came into Milton to sell basket-work and to tell fortunes.

Indeed, the summer before, when the Corner House girls and Neale O'Neil were at Pleasant Cove, they had had quite an experience with Gypsies—and not a very pleasant experience at that. Tess remembered this, though Dot did not; therefore the older sister was a little troubled as they approached the Gypsy encampment with the gaily dressed woman.

This opening in the woods, with a grassy road running through its center, which was plainly no main-traveled highway, was a lovely spot. The Gypsies are thorough exponents of the out-of-door life, now so much talked about; and they have, too, some idea of the beautiful and picturesque.

This encampment had been selected because of the pleasant little brook running near, and the real beauty of the spot. There were six big covered wagons, all brightly painted. Besides, four tents were set up, and there were coops of chickens and other signs that the encampment was more or less permanent.

On the appearance of the two strange little girls with the Gypsy woman, there was a rush of dogs, chickens, goats, pigs and children toward the newcomers. Tess and Dot clung together and tried to get behind the green and orange petticoat. The woman shouted something in a strange tongue, and drove the children and dogs back. The other curious riff-raff of the camp had to be actually kicked out of the path.

There were several cooking fires in the camp, a number of men and women in sight, and at least fifty horses grazing at one end of the park, watched by several half-grown youths. Plainly there was a big tribe of the Romany folk encamped in this spot.

The woman with the gay petticoat, having given up her basket of berries to a girl, led the visitors by the hand, one on either side, to the nearest fire, where a big man in brown velveteen garments, including a peaked cap, and wearing gold hoops in his ears and a heavy gold chain around his neck, was sitting in a green-painted easy chair.

This man was a person of much importance, it was evident. Nobody else came near him as the woman approached with the two little Corner House girls.

He was not a bad looking man at all, though his face was deeply graven in lines, and wind and weather had tanned his face and hands like leather. Again in that strange language which Tess and Dot did not know, the woman spoke to this man, who was certainly the leader of the Gypsies.

The man's eyes twinkled at the children, and he smiled. But he did not win their confidence. However, he shouted for another woman almost at once, and she came from the fire with two plates of steaming hot stew—either of rabbits or squirrels, Tess did not know which. And neither she nor Dot cared.

They were, indeed, very hungry. A diet of blueberries is not a filling one—especially when one has been without anything else to eat for so long as had the little Corner House girls. The woman with whom they had come into the camp sat down with them, having reported to the big man, and ate, too. They sat cross-legged on the grass, and had only spoons to eat with, and thick slices of very good ryebread to sop up the gravy of the stew. The woman said her name was Mira, and the children found her very pleasant and talkative.

"I wish our folks would come along in the automobile," Tess said, longingly, when their hunger was partly appeased.

"Do you s'pose they will come this way?" asked Dot of Mira.

"We shall see. He will 'tend to that," said the woman, coolly, nodding towards the big man in the chair.

Tess was very curious. "Who is he?" she asked, in a whisper. "Who is the man in the chair?"

"King David," said Mira.

"Oh!" gasped Dot. "I've heard of him. Didn't he play on a salt-cellar?"

"Oh, dear me!" cried Tess. "A 'psalter,' Dot—a 'psalter'!"

"Well, what's the difference?" asked the smallest Corner House girl, pouting.

"A good deal," declared Tess, although she had no idea herself just what a psaltery was, and was unaware that she had made a mistake quite as inexcusable as Dot's. "And, anyway," pursued Tess, whose confidence swamped her ignorance of the subject and duly impressed Dot, "anyway, this can't be the same King David."

"No," said the woman. "He is King David Stanley. We are English Gypsies."

"But—but you and he didn't talk English?" Tess suggested, hesitatingly.

"Among ourselves we talk Egyptian," said the woman, proudly. So she called the language of the Gypsies. "We are all Romany folk."

Of course, the children did not understand much about this. But Dot was anxious upon one point, and she whispered to Tess:

"How can that big man be a king? He doesn't wear a crown. Don't all kings wear 'em? I never saw a picture of a king without one on his head—though I should think 'twould make 'em bald."

"Sh!" whispered back Tess. "Maybe they aren't comfortable to wear."

"Well! where's his scalper?"

"His what?" gasped Tess.

"His scalper," declared Dot. "Kings always carry 'em in their hands."

"Oh, for mercy's sake!" ejaculated Tess. "A sceptre, you mean."

"Aren't they what kings scalp folks with?"

"Dear me, Dot Kenway!" said Tess, in despair. "Kings aren't like Indians. They don't scalp folks."

"But they order their heads cut off if they don't please 'em," said Dot, unconvinced, and eyeing King David askance.

The Gypsies were, however, all very kind to the visitors. Mira would not allow the wild and scantily dressed children of the camp to annoy the little Corner House girls. And she always drove the dogs away when they came too near, for Dot was frankly afraid of the hungry looking beasts.

But Mira brought a clothes-basket out of one of the tents, and covered in that were six little blind, black puppies, "too cute for anything," as Dot admitted. There were kittens, too, and a hutch of little chickens, and some tame rabbits. When the visiting children were shown two little kids—twins—gamboling around the mother goat, their delight knew no bounds.

These interests held their attention for much of the forenoon—especially Dot's. But Tess began to wonder if something would not soon be done about finding the automobile and their friends. She grew more anxious as noon approached and nothing was said about this mystery.

The King of the Gypsies had disappeared some time before. Mira was busy. And Dot, in spite of a lapful of kittens, began to ask her sister:

"Tess, when are we going to find Ruth and Aggie? I—I don't want to stay here much longer, do you?"

CHAPTER XV—ANOTHER CLUE

Neale O'Neil's early morning visit to the Gypsy camp had been very disappointing. The camp had been fully aroused, and there were plenty of children about; but none of these were Tess and Dot.

"But say!" Sammy Pinkney whispered to Neale in an awestruck voice, "you know how the Gypsies do when they steal kids, don't you? They stain 'em with walnut juice and you can't tell 'em then from their own kids."

"Well, I guess we should know Tess and Dot, if they were stained as black as Petunia Blossom's pickaninnies," snorted Neale. "The little girls aren't in this bunch, for sure!"

Meanwhile the constable had shown his star to King David Stanley and explained the errand they were here upon. The chief Gypsy vigorously denied having seen the lost children—as indeed he had not at that time—but he promised to look for them and have the tribe look in that vicinity immediately after breakfast.

"And if we find them you shall learn of it at once, young sir," the big Gypsy assured Neale. "I will myself bring you word at the village where you are stopping."

He spoke very good English, did the king, and seemed to be really sympathetic. But Neale O'Neil turned the automobile about, and with anxious heart drove back to Arbutusville.

They made him go to bed, once he arrived at the lodging where the older girls and Mrs. Heard were staying. Neale was completely worn out, and even Agnes refrained from letting him see how troubled and distraught they all were because of his non-success in finding Tess and Dot. Therefore, Neale was sound asleep when a man wearing brown velveteen and with gold rings in his ears rattled into town in a ramshackle old buggy, but behind a high-stepping horse. It was King David Stanley, and he hunted out Constable Munro at once and told him that the two lost children had been found and had been brought into the Gypsy camp.

Not being entirely sure that Tess and Dot were the two in which the automobile party were interested, the chief of the Romany tribe had judged it better to bring the news rather than the children.

"You know how our people are sometimes looked upon by the Gentiles," he said gravely. "If I had taken the little girls away from the camp, and their friends had appeared there, asking for them, my act in removing them would look suspicious."

"You're an all-right feller, if ye be a Gyp.," declared Mr. Munro, and he took King David over to the lodging where the automobile party was staying.

By this time the girls and Mrs. Heard were in the lowest depths of despair. Ruth was even seriously discussing sending a telegram to Mr. Howbridge.

"Though what he could do more than we are doing ourselves, I don't see," Mrs. Heard sighed.

"We are not doing anything!" cried Agnes, beginning to cry again. "I believe if they'd have let me go with them into the woods last night, I could have found poor, precious little Dot and Tessie. What shall we do——"

"I'll go with you, too, Aggie," declared Sammy, having hard work to keep back the tears himself. "I bet you and I can find 'em."

"It is the easiest thing in the world to be a critic," Ruth said quietly. "But we should first know how better to do a thing before finding fault with the person who has done it. I think——"

And just then Constable Munro and the big Gypsy appeared in their sitting-room, and immediately their despair was changed to joy. Neale came stumbling out of the bedroom, rubbing the sleep out of his eyes, and led the cheering. For a few moments the automobile tourists certainly were quite beside themselves.

Nothing would do but all must run out to the encampment to get the lost little girls. And although King David started before them, the motor car passed him and his swift pacer on the road and arrived at the Gypsy encampment a good fifteen minutes before he appeared.

Tess and Dot, by this time, had become rather lachrymose. They dared not ask Mira again about their lost friends; and even the lapful of kittens palled at last on Dot. With the coming of the automobile, however, all this was changed. At once both Tess and Dot could see nothing but good in their friends, the Gypsies. Ruth and Agnes, with Sammy, had to be led all about the encampment, to see the pets and to learn how the Gypsies lived in their wagons and tents, and otherwise to be shown the wonders of the place. Mrs.

Heard and Ruth ransacked their purses for pennies to distribute to the bare-legged children attached to the camp.

"And we were wild girls, too—for a little while," said Dot. "Weren't we, Tess?"

"Too bad you were so wild that I didn't find you when I was over this way early this morning," grumbled Neale O'Neil. "Anyway, if I hadn't insisted on coming we wouldn't have found the kids yet."

"My! aren't you smart?" scoffed Agnes, who felt happy enough to bicker with him now. "Well! somebody, I suppose, must blow a horn for you—why not yourself?"

"Oh, I don't make a practice of parading my virtues," began Neale, when Agnes stopped him with:

"I should say you didn't, Neale O'Neil. Let me tell you it takes quite a number to make a parade."

"Got me there! Got me there!" admitted the boy, grinning. He did not mind the tartness of his girl chum's tongue, now that the little ones were found. Everybody was joyful over the reunion.

The king of the Gypsies had been examining the automobile most curiously during this time.

"Fine car," he said to Neale. "I'm thinking some of getting one myself. Only trouble is, sure to frighten the horses, and if we didn't have horses to trade they wouldn't believe we were Gypsies," and he smiled with a wonderful flash of strong, white teeth.

Neale laughed. "I suppose pretty soon all up-to-date Gypsies will go about the country in auto-vans instead of those green and yellow painted wagons," he suggested.

"Mebbe," said the man. "We had a couple of men here one night not long ago with a car. They came from Milton. At least, I heard one of them say so."

Agnes was beside Neale. Suddenly she seized his arm and squeezed it tightly.

"Oh, Neale!" she gasped.

The boy had noted the significance of King David's speech too. He nodded to the girl and asked the big Gypsy at the same time:

"What sort of car did those fellows have?"

"Oh, it was a small car. A runabout—Maybrouke make. Good car, but not like this."

"Mr. Collinger's runabout," whispered Agnes. "That was his make."

"When were these fellows here?" asked Neale. Then he explained: "We're very much interested. One of our friends lost a car like the one you describe. Can you remember just when it was?"

"Oh, yes, young sir. It is fixed in my memory," and the Gypsy mentioned a date immediately following the day on which the car of the county surveyor had been taken away from the Milton court house.

"It was those men!" cried Agnes decidedly.

King David looked at her curiously. "They tried to sell the car to me," he said. "I was not sure they came by it honestly. So many people try to foist stolen goods on us because we are Gypsies."

This was a new light on that subject; yet Neale O'Neil thought it might be quite true. "Give a dog a bad name and hang him" is not only a trite saying, but a true one.

"What did the fellows look like?" he asked the chief, and quickly described in particular the fellow they knew as Saleratus Joe.

"No mistaking him, young sir," said the chief Gypsy. "He was one. The other was an older man."

"I don't know him so well," admitted Neale. "But I am sure it is lucky you did not buy the car. There would have been trouble. Do you know where they went from here?"

"No. They remained over night with us because a storm came up. I sheltered the car in one of our tents. But about a week ago I saw them and the car again," he added.

"No!" cried Neale, in surprise.

"Yes. I drove over into what they call the Fixville district—it's beyond Parmenter Lake—to look at a horse. There is a big farm over there that isn't being worked this year—owned by a man named Higgins. They're only getting the hay off it. You see, last winter the house burned to the ground and Mr. Higgins, who is an old man, was badly burned and isn't able yet to take up his work again. He is with friends somewhere. Well," went on the Gypsy, "the outbuildings and barns were saved. As I drove by the place I saw this freckled chap and that other backing the car into one of the big hay barns. It was just at nightfall. Of course, I don't know that they stayed there more than one night."

Neale and Agnes were greatly excited by this story. It seemed as though it were the clearest clue yet discovered regarding the stealing of Mr. Collinger's runabout. From the Gypsy Neale obtained a very clear and particular account of the place where the suspected men and car had last been seen, and how to get there.

"We'll just go around that way after we leave the hotel at Parmenter Lake," declared Agnes. "Why! maybe we'll find the car right there."

"It's too late for May bees," grinned Neale. "This is July."

But he had some little hope of tracing the lost car himself, in spite of his fun. However, as Mrs. Heard declared with decision, first of all the party would run on to the hotel at Parmenter Lake where they had rooms and their trunks awaiting them, and there recuperate.

"So much excitement is not good for me, I declare," said the lady. "I feel it in my legs."

That puzzled Dot Kenway immensely. Yet she was too polite to ask Mrs. Heard how it could be. Nevertheless, she whispered to Tess:

"How do you suppose she could feel our being lost in her legs? We did the walking."

Tess failed to give a satisfactory reply.

They arrived not long after mid-afternoon at the resort on Parmenter Lake, which was, indeed, a very popular inland summer place. Mrs. Heard felt the need of quietness, and Ruth spent most of her time watching the children; but Agnes felt no necessity for "recuperation."

She had a delightful time the two days and evenings they spent at the hotel. There was a dance each night, and she danced more than she ever had before in her life in forty-eight successive hours.

There were so many young people of about her age at the hotel and in neighboring cottages, that Agnes was sure to have her fill of enjoyment. Neale, meanwhile, overhauled the motor car and made all shipshape for their continued tour.

Tess and Dot lived in a sort of Land of Romance because of their recent adventure. They were much sought after by other little girls because they had been lost, had stayed in the woods all night, and had joined (if for only a brief time) a band of Gypsies.

Master Sammy was tipped out of a boat on the lake and came near drowning. Then he led a newly formed crew of "fresh water pirates" in a raid on an orchard and was caught and well spanked by the owner. He certainly was a trial; but he was growing strong and healthy looking. This outing was doing Sammy Pinkney a world of good, whether the older members of the touring party benefited or not.

When they finally left the Parmenter Lake hotel the motor car was in fine fettle and so were all the young people in it. And Mrs. Heard declared that her nerves had recovered from the shock they had suffered when Tess and Dot were lost.

Agnes and Neale, one may be sure, had not forgotten what King David Stanley had told them about Saleratus Joe and the missing runabout. They had heard nothing further about the stolen car, although both had asked.

Neale had looked up the roads in the guide book and they now sped directly over the nearest route for the abandoned farm where Joe and the car had last been observed by the Gypsy chief.

Mrs. Heard was quite as eager as Agnes and Neale to learn if trace of her nephew's car could be found in this neighborhood. She had written one letter to Mr. Collinger regarding their suspicions of Joe Dawson and his appearance with a runabout in this part of the State.

They ran on beyond the end of the lake and thence into a much more scantily populated country than that through which they had previously traveled.

They struck into the road at last on which King David had said the site of the burned farmhouse was. Not another dwelling was on this cross highway, and the road map gave its length as twelve miles.

Save for the cleared acres of the Higgins farm, on both sides thick woods bordered the road. Of course, they could not mistake the farm itself when they came to it. The fire had left nothing of the great house but the cellar walls.

However, there were several good outbuildings, especially the hay barns. The Gypsy had told Neale clearly into which of the two barns he had seen the men running the automobile.

"I'm going to have a squint, anyway," said Neale, stopping the car and promptly getting out.

"Be careful," urged Mrs. Heard. "Don't get into trouble," though how he could do that in this forsaken place it was not easy to guess.

There was not a soul around the place as far as the touring party could see.

CHAPTER XVI—SEARCHING THE BARN

"I'm going too! I'm going too!" exclaimed Sammy Pinkney, scrambling out of the car after Neale O'Neil.

Agnes was opening the door on her side of the car, but Neale said quietly:

"Now, wait a little, both of you. Aggie, you'd spoil everything. And, Sammy, you keep still," and he tossed that offended youngster back into the front seat.

"Aw, say!" bristled Sammy.

"You're so bossy, Neale O'Neil," declared Agnes. "I'd like to know——"

"See here," interrupted the youth, with his back to the burned house and the barns, "if there should be anybody on watch, it wouldn't do to let 'em see we'd come here just for the sake of looking into that hay barn."

"Oh!" observed Agnes, sitting down again.

Neale had opened the hood and made a pretense of fumbling inside.

"You see," he said, still in a low voice, "I want it to appear that something has happened to our car. Now I'm going to hunt in the tool kit——"

"Whuffor?" demanded Sammy. "I'll find it for you."

"You'll sit where you are," declared Neale O'Neil sternly. "I'm supposed to be hunting for something I can't find. Then I'll go up to that old barn and try to find it. It won't look right if everybody gets out of the car and goes snooping around."

"I admire your language, Neale O'Neil," sighed Ruth.

"Do go ahead and see what you can find, boy," urged Mrs. Heard, very much excited now.

"Goodness!" murmured Agnes. "He acts as though he expected to find that barn full of robbers."

"Nothin' but rats in it, I bet," grumbled Sammy, feeling much abused.

"Oh, there! You don't catch me going near it, then!" cried Agnes.

Neale, undisturbed by either Ruth's criticism or Agnes' fun-making, proceeded to act as though the motor car had really met with an accident. Finally he started for the barn, which stood some distance back from the road.

"Look out for the rats—oh, do look out for the rats, Neale!" Tess called after him.

"He can't whisper to the rats, anyway," remarked Dot. "I guess Neale O'Neil, even if he did come from a circus, can't tame all animals."

The approach to the barn was by a broad, well graveled drive which sloped smoothly upward to the wide barn door. Almost at once Neale O'Neil saw that there had been an automobile on this piece of gravel. He could see where the wheels had skidded and disturbed much of the surface of the drive—whether when the car entered the barn or when it came out, he could not say.

He looked sharply around on all sides, but saw nobody. By the strands of twisted hay hanging from the closed loft door he presumed the upper part of the barn was filled with the only crop being harvested on the Higgins farm this year. On trying the main door, Neale found it barred; but there was a small door beside the great one, and this opened at his touch upon the latch.

The great barn was filled with a brown dusk in which Neale O'Neil could see nothing at first. But by stepping within and leaving the door open, he was able to obtain some idea of what was on the barn floor. On either side were the mows, the hay stacked in them down to the ground. The loosely boarded loft over the runway of the barn had also been filled, he supposed. The sweet, dusty odor of the cured grasses was almost overpowering at first. Dim outlines of a few old agricultural tools were to be seen in the gloom. These were shoved back out of the way so as to clear the middle of the course.

Neale, still curious, fumbled at the bar which held closed the two-leaved door, and finally opened this. The door swung open slowly and the strong July sunlight rushed in. Millions of motes danced in the sunshine that spread across the barn floor. Now all was revealed.

"Can you find it?" cried Agnes from the seat of the automobile.

Neale had to wag his head in negation. There was nothing here that looked like a motor car. Back, at the rear of the barn floor, the hay had overflowed the mows and loft, and was heaped in a fragrant pile on the barn floor to the height of the floor of the loft.

"One sure thing, they've got an abundant hay crop stored away," thought Neale O'Neil. "Uncle Bill Sorber's elephants would find plenty of fodder here."

He laughed, barring the big doors again securely. As he came out of the barn he glanced sharply around, but saw nobody save his own friends in the motor car.

Naturally his examination of the other farm buildings was hasty; but he neglected to look into no shed large enough to have housed the runabout of which he was so eagerly in search. He came back to the Corner House automobile with the assurance that there was no car but their own at the Higgins farm, and made the statement boldly.

"Well, but," pouted Agnes, shaking her head at him, "I'd feel much more satisfied if you had let me look."

"Me, too," grumbled Sammy. "I bet I could see into smaller places than you could, Neale O'Neil."

Neale just grinned at them. "This isn't a flivver we are looking for, I'd have you know. The Maybrouke is some car, believe me! You folks talk like the funny-man who went into the flivver factory to look around; and when he came out he kept scratching himself—said he was sure he had got one of the things on him!"

There was no use of waiting around on this lonely road any longer, so Neale got in and started the car again. As they had got off their original route some distance in coming to this farm, it would be impossible to make a good hotel that night.

"But," as Mrs. Heard said, "we have nothing to fear after that lodging in Frog Hollow——"

"Arbutusville, Mrs. Heard—do!" laughed Agnes, in correction.

"Well. That woman had the hardest beds I ever saw. If the street pavements had been as hard they would certainly have had good roads in that town."

They stopped at a countryside store for lunch and bought crackers and cheese and milk, and feasted while sitting in the automobile under the shade of a great elm.

"We're almost like Gypsies ourselves," said Tess, ruminating as she crunched the crackers and cheese. "Aren't we, Dot?"

"No. We're cleaner," said the smallest Corner House girl; "and we haven't any little goaties—and pigs! But this is lots of fun, just the same; and I wish we could sleep out again all night—just for once—all of us, of course."

She came near having her wish that very night, or so it seemed when sunset came. In some way they got off the marked route they had been following, and, on stopping at a crossroads to ask a blacksmith who was just closing his shop, they found that they were far away from the beaten track of automobile tourists.

"We might have known that," grumbled Ruth, "from the state of the roads."

"The worst of it is," said Mrs. Heard, a little worried, "it is going to be hard on the children. They are tired out now. And it is a dark night."

"No moon till late—that's a fac', ma'am," said the blacksmith, leaning on the mud-guard while Neale lit the lamps.

"And have we got to go back over that rocky piece of road to get to the Tailtown Pike?" asked Agnes, trying to study out the lost route in the guide book.

"It's forty-five miles to Tailtown, where we were going to stop. And over the meanest roads in the State, I bet," growled Neale.

"Dear me!" sighed Ruth.

"There are some objections to touring the country roads in an automobile," admitted Mrs. Heard. "And things seemed to be going so smoothly!"

"I dunno what you'll do," drawled the blacksmith. "'Nless you talk to mother."

"To whom?" chorused the older girls and the chaperone.

"Mother. Mebbe she kin advise ye," drawled the man. "We live down the road jest a piece. I dunno what she'd say——"

"Does she know the roads better than you do?" asked Neale bluntly.

The blacksmith laughed mellowly. "I don't reckon she does—'cept the road to Heaven, son," he said. "She sure knows all about that. But she might be helpful. I've been takin' her advice, off and on, for forty years, and whenever I've took it I've not been sorry."

"Come!" exclaimed Ruth suddenly, "let us drive on to this gentleman's house."

"Where is it?" asked Neale, getting in behind the steering wheel again.

"You can see our kitchen lamp twinkling in the window yonder," said the blacksmith, stepping upon the running-board as Neale started the car.

They jolted down the rough road, and quickly came to the house in question. As far as they could see, it was rather a large country house with a terraced lawn before it and a driveway running up beside the dwelling to the rear premises.

"Drive her right up to the door, young man," advised the blacksmith.

"Room to turn around up there?" asked Neale, the careful.

"Plenty," agreed the man. "Don't have no fear about that."

Neale immediately turned the car up the little incline and the blacksmith leaped to the ground as it stopped.

"Now," he said jovially, "one of you young misses just go up there on the porch and tell mother how you're fixed. You can git out, ma'am, I'm sure," he added, to Mrs. Heard, as Ruth jumped from the car. "Get out your baggage too—this here little shaver can help at that," and he rumpled Sammy's hair with his big hand.

"But—but——Do you mean we can stay here?" gasped Mrs. Heard.

Ruth had scarcely reached the door when it was opened from within. A comfortable figure of a woman, with spectacles and gray hair, faced the oldest Corner House girl.

"Well, well!" said "Mother," in just the hearty tone of voice a mother should possess. "An automobile party? Well, well! how many of you air there, my dear?"

"But, my goodness me!" gasped Ruth. "You're not going to take us in 'sight unseen,' in this way, are you?"

The woman laughed. "Why not?" she asked. "If you are going to do anything for anybody, it ain't perlite to hem and haw about it, I'm sure. Leastways, that's the way I was brought up, my dear. And there's little children with you, too! Of course you shall stay."

Ruth and the others were speechless. Such hospitality—and evidently this was not a house of public entertainment—was quite unexpected.

"That you, Buckley?" she called to her husband. "You see to putting up the car. How many did you say there was? I want to know how much ham to slice," and she chuckled unctuously again.

"There's seven of 'em, Mother," called the blacksmith's mellow voice from the dark, "and a dog. B'sides, mebbe you'd better take notice that two of 'em's boys, and like enough they've got their appetites with 'em," and he broke into another mellow guffaw.

"Well," Agnes later whispered to Ruth, "this is certainly the unexpected end of a perfect day! Goodness! what should we have done if these good people hadn't taken us in? The blacksmith says they are rebuilding the bridge over Mason's Creek and we couldn't have got across."

"Oh!"

"And that would have made us go around so far that the run to Tailtown would have been nearer sixty miles than forty-five."

They were all glad; and such a supper of ham and eggs as they ate! The accommodations the blacksmith's wife put at the party's disposal were ample too.

"Just the same," yawned Neale, before retiring, "this has sure been an empty day. There hasn't been much doing."

"Well, what do you expect to happen in these perfectly civilized places?" responded Agnes.

"And we have surely had enough excitement to last us for a while—the children getting lost, and all," Ruth said.

"And you hunted for that car of Mr. Collinger's," said Agnes, slyly. "That was exciting, I'm sure."

"Oh—ouch!" yawned Neale. "Don't knock, Aggie. We may find that car—and Saleratus Joe—yet."

"Your desire for low company shocks me, Neale," giggled Agnes. "Saleratus Joe, indeed!"

"Don't say a word," the boy retorted. "You and Ruth met the gentleman first—don't forget that," and they separated for the night with laughter.

CHAPTER XVII—ONE THING AFTER ANOTHER

Things began to happen, however, bright and early the next morning. "The kids," as Neale called the two smaller Corner House girls and Sammy Pinkney, were out of their beds betimes, and out of doors as soon as they were dressed. The blacksmith's house was an old-fashioned place, and there were many things interesting to the little folks about it. Besides, if there had not been a thing in sight, the three juveniles would have dug up something interesting in a very short time.

The blacksmith was already off to start his smithy fire in the shop at the fork of the roads. "Mother," with the help of a neighbor's daughter called in for this emergency, was hurrying about the kitchen and dining room preparing the huge breakfast she thought necessary for these unexpected guests.

Neale O'Neil came out, yawning as he had gone to bed, and opened the door of the shed in which the automobile had been lodged in lieu of a proper garage. Neale always looked over the car before they started the day's run, as all careful chauffeurs should.

The children ran for the automobile, of course, before Neale could back it out of the shed; and as Tess and Dot and Sammy jumped on the steps to ride out, a white hen flew from the tonneau with a wild squawk.

"Oh, for goodness' sake!" cried Tess. "What do you s'pose that hen was doing there?"

The hen had flown to the top rail of the calf pen, and there proceeded to "cut, cut, cu-da-cut!" just as loud as she could.

"Aw, what are you squalling about?" Sammy demanded. "Nobody hurt you."

"Maybe she wants to go to ride with us in our automobile," said Dot demurely.

When the automobile was backed out upon the gravel it was Tess who looked into the tonneau and spied the reason for Mrs. White Hen's loud remarks. There it lay, white and warm, upon the rear seat.

"Goodness! Goodness me!" gasped Tess, with clasped hands. "Isn't that cunning? She laid an egg right here for us, Dot."

"My," Dot observed, "maybe she thought she could pay for a ride with us."

"I guess she must know something about the way gas has gone up," chuckled Neale O'Neil, "and she wanted to pay for her share."

They had to secure that egg at once and run to ask "mother" if they could have it. Though, as Dot Kenway declared:

"It's the most mysteriousest thing why that blacksmith calls her 'mother' when she isn't, but she's his wife."

However, that "mysteriousest thing" was not on the carpet just then. It was the egg found in the automobile that was in question, and the blacksmith's wife said:

"Yes, of course you shall have it. Them dratted hens lay everywhere. I guess they'd lay in the parson's hat."

"Oo-oo! not if he had it on," murmured Dot.

Then immediately, there was another subject of discussion. What should they do with the fresh-laid egg?

"Eat it, of course," said Sammy.

"It won't go far—one egg—among three such savage appetites as you kids possess," Neale declared.

"Why—no," murmured Tess. "You couldn't very well divide an egg in three parts."

"Not till it's cooked," Sammy put in, promptly. "Let's have it fried."

"Oh! I like eggs soft-boiled," Dot exclaimed.

"Why! then we can't divide it even after it's cooked," cried Tess; "for I like my eggs hard-boiled."

"It can't be done, then," said Neale O'Neil, solemnly, but vastly amused. "You can't first boil an egg hard, and then soft, and then fry it."

"She—she ought to have laid three eggs," growled Sammy.

"You should speak to her about that," Neale returned. Then he added, as a suggestion: "Why don't you cast lots for it?"

"Cast lots for what, Neale O'Neil!" demanded Dot, wonderingly.

"Is—isn't that wicked—like gambling?" asked Tess, slowly, "or playing marbles for keeps?"

"No," Neale told her, "I don't believe it is. You can take three straws of different lengths. I'll hold 'em. The one that draws the longest straw takes the egg—and can have it cooked any way she or he pleases."

"But then the others won't get any," wailed Dot, whose appetite was evidently sharpened by the morning air.

"Shucks!" said Neale, washing his hands of the matter. "Give it to Tom Jonah, then. He'll eat it raw—shell and all."

"Oh, no," said Tess, with sudden inspiration. "We must give it to Mrs. Heard for her breakfast. I'll ask the blacksmith's wife to cook it."

That suited everybody and Tess and Dot ran to make the proper culinary arrangements for the wonderful egg laid on the automobile seat.

It was a very hilarious breakfast, indeed; and the older girls and Mrs. Heard thought the "automobile egg" quite wonderful indeed. And such a breakfast as it was—with eggs galore, and fried chicken, and hot bread, and honey from "Mother's own combs."

When Dot heard that, she was puzzled a good deal at first, for all the comb she had seen about the blacksmith's wife was a high-backed, old-fashioned tortoise-shell comb that was prominent in the woman's "bob" of hair. It had to be explained to the smallest Corner House girl what "honey from the comb" meant. All of that succulent dainty Dot had ever seen before had been strained honey.

The blacksmith's wife put up a hamper of lunch for the automobile tourists, too, and when they drove away at nine o'clock the Corner House girls and their companions felt as though they were bidding good-bye to two old and valued friends. It did not seem possible that they had never met the jolly blacksmith and his kindly wife before the previous evening; and they promised to stop again, if only to call, on their return journey.

"I'm sure we shall never forget the dears," Agnes sighed, some hours later, when they had stopped for lunch. "Just look at all this fried chicken!"

"We won't forget 'Mother' while the grub holds out, that's sure," grinned Neale O'Neil.

"Horrid boy!" retorted Agnes. "We girls, I should hope, think of something besides our stomachs."

"Hm—yes. But you weren't talking about anything else," rejoined Neale.

The party had another subject of thought the next moment, however. Neale was just setting up the tripod, and Sammy was scurrying about for dry wood for the fire to be built under it, when a tall and roughly dressed man broke through the brush into the open patch of turf on which the party was preparing camp, and at once hailed them:

"Hey, you! what are ye doing here, I'd like to know?"

Neale took it upon himself to reply—and he did not feel very pleasant about it. The man did not speak in a nice way.

"I don't know that it's any of your affair," the boy said quietly; "but we are just preparing lunch."

"Oh, you be?" snarled the fellow. "Wal, by jinks! ye ben't neither! We don't want no ortermobile parties here. Get out!"

"Do you own this land?" asked Neale, his voice shaking.

"Never mind him. Come away—do!" cried Ruth to Neale, while she retreated to the car, dragging the hamper with her.

"I hate to do that," said the boy, who was very angry. "I don't believe he has any right to send us away. We're doing no harm."

"Ye air trespassin'," declared the man. "Going to build a fire, too, was ye? That's against the law, anyway."

"To build a campfire?" demanded Neale, quickly. "I guess not. And you've got to prove trespass."

"I'll prove it with the flat o' my hand on your ears, ye young rascal!" declared the man, hotly. "You ain't paid anybody for the right to camp here, have you?"

"Paid anybody? Of course not. Who'd we pay?" demanded Neale, still inclined to stand his ground.

"Shows ye don't know the law in this town," said the man, with satisfaction. "I'm a consterble—see?" and he threw back his coat and showed a big, shiny star pinned to his "gallus." "I got the authority."

"You've got the authority to what?" asked Neale, sourly. "Trying to tree us for a collection, are you? I—guess—not!"

"Oh, Neale," begged Ruth. "Do come away."

"The boy is right," said Mrs. Heard, vigorously. "I believe the man is overstepping his rights. But we don't want to fight him here. Oh! what is that child about?"

Sammy Pinkney had procured several smooth pebbles of about the size of hen's eggs, and now approached the contending parties. Tom Jonah, too, stood beside Neale and began to show his remaining fangs.

"What are you going to do with those stones, Sammy Pinkney?" demanded Agnes.

"Goin' to give some of 'em to Neale if he wants 'em," declared the youngster, with a grin.

Neale O'Neil laughed at that. "I guess we won't come to blows, Sammy," he said. "We'll just get in the car and have our lunch. This constable can't keep us from eating on the county road, that is sure. Get out the alcohol lamp, folks, if you want your tea."

They put up the board, and unlimbered the lamp and soon had the kettle boiling; but the constable sat down near by and watched them—and with no pleasant face—the while. Evidently, although they had obeyed his command, he was not wholly satisfied.

It was while they were still eating their lunch that the sky became overcast.

"It really looks as though we should have a tempest, and we ought to get under cover," remarked Mrs. Heard.

"Oh, yes, do!" said Agnes, eagerly. "I dislike getting drenched."

They were some distance on the road to Tailtown, however, before the first flash of lightning assured them that the storm was going to overtake them before they could reach any haven.

Neale stopped immediately and put up the top and drew the curtains on either side. He made Agnes get back into the tonneau, although that crowded the others somewhat. But under the rubber blanket in front there was scarcely room for Sammy, Neale, and Tom Jonah.

The rain began drumming on the top of the car before they started again. They were in a locality where there seemed to be no farms. At least they had not passed a barn within the hour that promised shelter for the car. So it was better to go ahead and risk it, than to run back.

CHAPTER XVIII—A VERY ANNOYING SITUATION

In a minute or two the rain was falling torrentially—beating upon the automobile cover and quickly turning the sandy road to an actual mire.

It grew rapidly dark, although it was only mid-afternoon. Overhead the lightning crackled and the thunder ricochetted from the distant hills. The trees bordering the road swayed in the wind and the weight of the falling rain bent them like saplings.

Neale O'Neil could not drive the automobile rapidly, much as they desired to reach a place of refuge from the storm, for the wind-shield was blurred so that he had to poke his head out at the side every now and then to watch the road.

The roar of the elements was appalling. The girls and Mrs. Heard shut their eyes and cowered in the tonneau when the sharp flashes of lightning came. But they were perfectly dry.

Sammy was in a state of hysterical delight. He was not frightened, but he jumped every time the thunder broke above them. Once Neale told him to keep still, but Sammy cried:

"I can't, Neale. I don't mean to jump—and I wouldn't if it wasn't for that old thunder. I know the bolt of lightning I see won't hit me—my dad told me that. I guess if I was deaf so I wouldn't hear the thunder, I'd keep as still as still!"

Not much was said by the girls, and Tom Jonah merely hung his pink tongue out like a flag, whining sometimes when the thunder rolled; for, like Sammy, he was mostly disturbed by it.

The narrow road ahead, as they swooped down into a hollow, seemed to be flooded. The shallow gutters could not contain the amount of water which had fallen, and the wheels of the automobile rolled through a brown stream of sand and water. At the bottom of this hill was a sharp turn; but Neale saw this in plenty of time. However, what lay beyond was completely hidden by an outthrust bank. The water in the driveway deepened as they descended. Despite the hard going the automobile gained momentum from the descent, and Neale steered carefully.

"Just like riding through a river, ain't it, Neale?" shrieked Sammy.

Tom Jonah, as excited as Sammy himself, barked. Neale punched the horn, although he did not expect to meet anybody or anything in such a storm and in such a lonely place. He slipped in the clutch at the bottom of the hill, turning out slightly to make the turn. He could not foresee the result of this last move; but he realized his mistake in just ten seconds—when it was too late.

The rear wheels skidded a little, and then the car, on the right side, slumped down into the mud and water, hub deep, and stopped dead!

The girls screamed, and Mrs. Heard, too, was frightened by the sudden jolt and the way the car tipped over. It did seem for a moment or two as though there might be a complete overturn.

"Now you've done it, Neale O'Neil!" cried Agnes, in her excitement.

"I s'pose I made it rain, too," sniffed Neale, in disgust. "You give me a pain, Aggie."

"What nonsense to blame Neale," Ruth, the fair-minded, hastened to put in. "What shall we do?"

"Stay where we are and keep dry," Mrs. Heard declared, with decision.

"But Neale can't get the car out of the mud with us in it," Agnes cried.

"Nor with you out of it, I reckon," said the boy, crossly; "wait till I see."

He crawled out with some difficulty to look the situation over, having to drive back Sammy and Tom Jonah with decision. "I don't want you two ramping around out here," he growled.

Neale had put on his slicker when the downpour began, and it was well he had, for this was no ordinary rain. The rush of water had filled the gutter with sand in solution, and there was now a regular quagmire where the wheels of the automobile stood. The fury of the storm had somewhat relaxed, but the rain fell steadily. Even should the rain stop, the water would not run out of this spot for hours. It did not take "half an eye," as Neale himself said, to see that they were stuck.

"And this is a nice place to spend the night in," complained Agnes.

"Can nothing really be done, Neale?" asked Mrs. Heard, much worried.

"I can't get her out without help," admitted the boy, in a discouraged tone.

Tess and Dot were crying a little, and Sammy looked at them scornfully. "Aw, you kids make me sick," he said. "You don't see me bawling, do you? S'pose you was in a pirate ship, 'way out in the ocean, and she was wrecked?"

"I don't want to be a pirate—so there!" sobbed Dot.

Tess said, solemnly: "Wait till you get hungry, Sammy Pinkney."

This silenced Sammy—for the time being, at least.

Suddenly Agnes cried aloud: "Oh, dear me! here it comes again."

It certainly sounded as though the tempest were returning, there was such a rattling and jangling behind them on the hill. Neale ran around the automobile to look.

A big wagon with a tarpaulin over it, making it look as large as a load of hay, and drawn by a pair of drenched horses, came rattling down the hill. There were two figures in slickers and rubber hats on the seat under the hood.

"A tin peddler's outfit, sure as you live," he cried.

"Oh, dear, Neale," said Ruth, "maybe they will be rough men and will not help you."

"I reckon they'll help us if we make it worth their while," said the boy, with assurance, peering through the rain to try to make out the faces of the two on the wagon seat.

"Be careful, boy," said Mrs. Heard. "Don't show them much money. We don't know what sort of men they may be. Peddlers——"

Neale reached back into the car and seized a heavy wrench. "Nothing like 'preparedness,'" he said, with a grin.

"My goodness!" exclaimed Agnes, giggling suddenly, "they'll think you are a highway robber."

"I'm going to hold them up all right," returned Neale O'Neil, with assurance.

The wagon was evidently hung with a large supply of tinware and the like, but all under the canvas cover. Yet it came down the hill at such a pace that the horses must not have found their load a heavy one to draw.

Of course the two strangers saw Neale, and the stalled car could not be overlooked, either. The one driving pulled in his team. Neale could make out the features of neither, for the turned-down brims of their hats hid their faces.

But the one driving called out in a very pleasant and unexpectedly cultivated voice:

"Hello there! What's the matter? In a hole?"

"That's just what we are in," Neale responded, and immediately tossed the wrench back into the car. He knew they had nothing to fear from a man with a voice like that.

"Is she in deep?" asked the stranger.

"You can see how she's bogged down," Neale returned. "No chance of my humping her out under her own engine, that's sure."

"You need something more—about two-horse power, eh?" said the driver of the peddler's cart, with a laugh.

"It must be a very annoying situation," said the second person on the seat of the cart.

Neale fairly jumped. It was a most astonishing thing, and he gaped impolitely for a moment up into the speaker's face. It was a girl!

Neale O'Neil was sure that she laughed at his surprise. But the young man said nothing further as he wrapped the lines around the whipstock and began to climb down.

By this time the Corner House girls were peering out of the curtains of the automobile, very much interested. The young man, when he got upon the ground, appeared to be about twenty-one, and his face was keen and pleasant, if not handsome. It seemed very queer indeed to find two young people of this character driving a tin peddler's wagon through the country.

"It is a girl!" whispered Agnes, shrilly. "Goodness me! what fun!"

"And a nice girl, too," murmured Ruth. "That man looks like a college student."

"Do you s'pose they are on their honeymoon?" suggested the romantic Agnes.

"For pity's sake don't ask them till you are a little better acquainted," begged Ruth.

Mrs. Heard asked the strange girl: "Won't you get wet up there?"

"Oh, no; I'm quite dry, thanks. And then I can go inside the wagon if it gets too rough."

Not only Mrs. Heard, but the girls expressed their surprise at this statement.

"You see," explained the girl, "we have the cart fixed like a van inside. We can sleep in it if we don't want to put up our tent. It's very cozy indeed."

"Why," said Mrs. Heard, "this seems to be an entirely new idea. And do you really peddle tinware?"

"Oh, yes. Just like other peddlers. Only the country people would rather trade with us, for we look honest," and she laughed merrily. "Besides, we did it last summer, too, and almost everybody remembers us in this country."

"I should think it would be splendid!" cried Agnes, with her usual enthusiasm over anything new.

"Oh, yes; it's fine. And we are having a nice vacation, Luke and I. Luke is my brother. Luke Shepard. I am Cecile."

Ruth at once gave in turn the names of the automobile party. Meanwhile Dot said to Tess:

"I guess she knows how to be a wild girl better'n you and me did," and Tess agreed, though with a whispered protest over her sister's grammar.

Neale and young Mr. Shepard had finally decided that the only way to get the car out of the mire was to unhitch the team from the peddler's wagon and use that "two horse power engine."

"You'll all have to get out while it's being done, too," said Neale to his party. "There'll be weight enough for one pair of horses, at best."

At once Cecile Shepard hopped down from the seat of the cart, and while the boys unhitched the horses, she got an umbrella and took Mrs. Heard first from the automobile to the rear of the van. There were steps and a door which gave entrance to the strange vehicle; and a lamp was quickly lighted inside. Then Cecile came back with the umbrella for the girls, and the entire touring party, save Neale and Tom Jonah, but including Sammy, were soon cozily ensconced in the peddler's wagon.

The Corner House girls were delighted with the way the van was arranged—and they were delighted with the cheerful, intelligent Cecile Shepard, too. They had a very talkative time while the boys worked hard to get the stranded automobile out of the mud.

The rain thundered down upon the huge tarpaulin that covered the van. A sweet breath of damp air blew through the wagon from the opening in front to the open door behind. Cecile told them something of the experiences of herself and her brother as tin peddlers.

Luke had a rope long enough to surround the body of the stalled automobile, so that the strain could be properly distributed. He and Neale tackled on the horses and carefully started them.

At the second trial the automobile wheels came out of the mud, and she rolled out upon the harder center of the road.

"Whoop—ee!" yelled Neale. "Now we're all right. And—and the rain is stopping! What do you know about that?"

CHAPTER XIX—THE TIN BADGE OF THE LAW

"The roads will be full of mudholes for miles," said Luke Shepard. "Never mind if it does stop raining, it will be bad traveling for an automobile. You see, I know this section of the country pretty well."

"Cracky!" groaned Neale. "We may get into another mess, then."

"You're likely to do so," agreed Luke. "Of course, by morning, if it rains no more, the water will have practically all run off. The roads being sandy hereabout they soon dry out."

"And meanwhile we'll be running risks every mile," growled Neale O'Neil.

"Every rod," said Luke, smiling.

"Cracky! but you're a cheerful fellow," said the boy from Milton. "Don't let the girls hear you say it. Agnes, especially. She'll go up in the air."

"You'd better take shelter with us, then," proposed the young tinware peddler.

"How's that?" asked Neale, curiously. "Not in that party-wagon of yours? We'd sure be a 'close corporation.'"

"Oh, no!" and the other laughed. "We're going to Alonzo Keech's barn. It's up a side road a piece—just around this turn. That's where sis and I were heading for. You see," Luke Shepard further explained, "we have established a regular route for our wares, and we have been here before—and put up at Keech's barn, too."

Meanwhile Cecile Shepard had suggested the same thing to Mrs. Heard and the Corner House girls. They all agreed to this, for to the automobile touring party it was "any port in a storm."

The boys rehitched the span of very good horses to the peddler's wagon, Luke got on the driver's seat and the girls and Sammy returned to the automobile, and the procession started, the peddler's wagon going ahead to lead the way.

Neale was very careful to keep in the middle of the road thereafter; for although the rain had ceased, as Luke foretold, the roads were still rivers. The branch road they turned into led back in the same general direction from which the tourists had come; but that made no difference now. It was shelter for the night they wanted, and in the on-coming darkness and the storm they all felt only too glad to be led without question.

In a half hour or so, they came out of the woods, after surmounting a hill, and found open fields all about them. The sky remained overcast and it was a dark night; but it was better here in the open than in the woods where the accident to the automobile had happened. There was not a gleam of lamplight anywhere; and when the peddler's wagon stopped finally in front of a great hay barn, Luke Shepard assured them that the dwelling of the owner of the farm was beyond a patch of woods and could not be seen even in daylight.

"I hope he will not object to our stopping here," Mrs. Heard said, when she climbed down from the van, in which she had stayed for the ride to the barn.

"Yes. We have had one experience with the natives," Agnes said, laughing, "that was not pleasant."

"Oh! Mr. Keech will not object," Cecile assured them. "We have found the people around here very nice indeed."

"So have we—for the most part," Ruth hastened to say. "Nobody could be nicer than the people we stayed with last night"; and she told the Shepards about the blacksmith and "Mother."

"Oh, we know them! They are the salt of the earth!" cried Cecile.

"Then that constable that wouldn't let us eat our lunch in the woods over yonder must be the pepper," said Neale, with a grin.

Luke and Cecile had to be told about that. But they did not recognize the officious constable.

"He must be a new one, and feels his oats," said Luke.

"I think he was a cheap grafter and wanted to be tipped," said Neale O'Neil. "That's what I think."

"But of course he was an officer of the law," Mrs. Heard said. "He wore a badge."

"'The tin badge of courage,'" said Luke with a laugh. "I don't know who he could be. But this Mr. Keech who owns this place is the county sheriff. So we have the law on our side while we stop here. Mr. Keech is our friend. We shall stop at his house to-morrow and spend most of the day. We always do when we get around this way."

The door of the barn was found unbarred, and with the automobile lights and Luke's lanterns, the party "made camp" very nicely indeed. The automobile was backed in on the floor of the barn, and the big doors left open. The Shepards' tent—a very good wall tent—was erected on a well-drained piece of ground. It was decided that Mrs. Heard and the girls should sleep in the tent and in the van, while the male members of the two parties put back the motor car cover and made themselves comfortable on the cushioned seats of the car.

Of course, supper came before this scheme of retiring had been adjusted. And a delightful time they had getting the meal and eating it. The food was mostly supplied by the "tin peddlers," as Agnes insisted upon calling Luke and Cecile Shepard.

"I shall lay in some condensed foods myself just as soon as we find a town again," declared Mrs. Heard. "These chances of being caught in lonely places without anything to eat come too frequently. Touring the country in a motor car is not very different from being cast away on a desert island!"

The children, of course, thought the experience quite as exciting as anything that had previously occurred.

"I like it better than the Gypsy camp," said Dot, warmly. "That cart we are going to sleep in is just the cutest thing."

"Just the same, I am glad Tom Jonah is with us this time," Tess said. "Everything is so sort of open around here."

The presence of the big dog made them all feel safer when the time to retire came, although the Shepards were used to camping out, and had never yet been molested in their two years' experience.

The two parties gave each other full personal particulars. The brother and sister had friends in Milton, whom the Corner House girls knew. And then, there was another bond between Luke and Cecile Shepard and the four Corner House girls. They were all orphans.

Luke was in his sophomore year at college. Cecile was attending a preparatory school, and was going to have a college education, too. But they had partly to work for it, for their only relative was a maiden aunt who could help them but little, and there had been only money enough left by their mother to partly educate the brother and sister.

"And we get a nice vacation and lots of fun and some money by going out with our van for three months each year," Cecile explained. "The rest of the year we rent the horses and van and the route to a man who has a little restaurant business at the shore in the summer. So we do pretty well."

Tom Jonah, as watchman, made no sound all night long. The weather gradually cleared, and at daybreak there was every promise of a beautiful day, with everything washed clean by the rain.

The motoring party decided to make an early start—and without breakfast. The Shepards knew just where there was a good roadside hotel only twenty miles away, and Neale was sure they would get there in season for breakfast.

Their host and hostess, however, insisted upon their having coffee before they started, and when the automobile got under way, the Corner House girls and their party felt, as they had the morning previous, that they were leaving some very good friends behind. They hoped to meet Luke and Cecile again on their return trip; if not, Cecile was to write to Ruth. The "tin peddlers" had also promised to make the old Corner House, in Milton, a visit during the next winter.

"Dear me suz!" sighed Agnes, as they wheeled away, using one of Mrs. MacCall's exclamations, "isn't this just delightful? I think touring the country in this way, and meeting folks, and making friends, is just delightful."

"Not so delightful last night when that storm was beating down upon us," Mrs. Heard reminded her.

"And you did your share of the kicking then, all right all right," put in Neale O'Neil. "Oh, you did squall, Aggie."

"Horrid thing!" exclaimed Agnes. "Don't remind me of unpleasant things this morning. I feel—I feel as happy as a big sunflower."

Just then they turned a curve in the level road and saw a lanky man in a drooping-brimmed hat, standing in the middle of the way.

"Hul-lo!" ejaculated Neale, slowing down.

"Is the man deaf?" demanded Mrs. Heard.

Neale punched the horn a couple of times, and the man merely turned to face them and held up a warning hand.

"Oh, cracky!" cried Neale. "Another tin-badger."

"And he's holding one of those tin watches on us, too," said Agnes, in despair.

"Say!" observed Sammy, the sharp-eyed. "That's the cop that wouldn't let us build the fire yesterday."

"It certainly is," gasped Ruth. "Now what shall we do?"

"I feel like bumping him," growled Neale. Nevertheless, he shut off the engine as the constable seemed to have no intention of moving out of the road.

"Wal!" said the tall man, finally facing them completely and snapping the case of his watch shut in a very business-like way. "Got ye that time, I swan! Comin' fifty mile an hour if ye was an inch——"

Suddenly he discovered that he was not entirely a stranger to the touring party. His mouth sagged open for a moment and he did not continue his remarks before Neale got in a word or two.

"You are very much mistaken, constable," he said. "I could not drive this car on this road at the speed you state—and if you knew anything about an auto you'd know it, too."

"Oh, don't, Neale!" whispered Ruth, from behind.

"So! I've seen ye before, have I, young cock o' the walk?" snarled the constable. "You was running over speed, an' don't you fergit it. And I'm goin' to take ye all back to Tuckerville and let Jedge Winslow tell ye sumpin'."

"Oh, dear me!" moaned Agnes. "And we haven't had breakfast!"

Mrs. Heard here put in her word—and she spoke sternly:

"You are making a grave mistake, Mr. Officer. We do not drive our automobile at any time faster than the law allows. And certainly we were not doing so now. How do you know how fast we were coming? You could not even see us until we came around that curve."

"Oh, I've had experience, I have, ma'am," said the fellow with a mean grin on his homely face.

"This is a regular hold-up!" exclaimed Neale, in wrath. "Why didn't you pull a gun and tell us to hold up our hands while you went through our pockets? It wouldn't be any worse."

"I'm likely to pull me a good switch an' wear it out on ye, ye fresh Ike!" declared the constable. "Don't you hand me no more sass—now I warn ye."

"But to go away back to Tuckerville!" groaned Ruth.

"And not a hotel there," Agnes said.

"I do not believe any justice of the peace will uphold this fellow if we do appear before him," Mrs. Heard said.

"If ye don't want to go," said the constable, whose ears seemed to be as preternaturally keen as they were unnaturally large—"if ye don't want to go back to Tuckerville, ye kin pay yer fine right here—ten dollars. That'll be about right, unless I add on a coupla dollars more to pay for this boy's sass."

"What did I tell you?" exclaimed Neale, to the others. "It's a hold-up!"

CHAPTER XX—EXCITEMENT

Neale O'Neil may not have been very wise in talking so plainly in the hearing of the mean-spirited fellow; but he could not be blamed for being indignant. It was positive that the Corner House girls' automobile had not been speeding when the man with the badge stopped it. And now his demand for ten dollars showed plainly that his petty mind was interested only in getting money easily rather than in enforcing the law.

"You'd better keep a civil lip on you, young man," said the constable, scowling at Neale. Then to Mrs. Heard he added: "Come now, lady, you can pay the fine to me and drive on; or you can go back to Tuckerville under arrest and pay it to Jedge Winslow. Take yer ch'ice."

"Oh, dear me!" whispered Agnes. "Let's give him the money and go on to the hotel Cecile Shepard told us about. Tuckerville, they say, is an awful place."

"Yes. Pay him the ten dollars—do, Mrs. Heard," Ruth urged the chaperone.

"Very well," said the lady. "I disapprove of such a thing, but it at least will relieve us of this man's presence——"

"Here comes another car," cried Tess, who was not wholly attentive to the argument.

"Now you'll get a chance to sting another party," snapped Neale, glaring at the constable.

But the latter made him no reply. In fact, he had suddenly changed his attitude. Instead of standing boldly before the machine, he cringed along to the tonneau door with his hand held out for the money Mrs. Heard was selecting from her bag.

"Hold on!" exclaimed Neale, suddenly. "Don't pay that fellow too quickly. Let's have witnesses. Here comes the car."

"You pay me now, or 'twill be too late," cried the constable, angrily.

Just then the coming car appeared around the curve—a heavy roadster. The plainly frightened constable gave the single occupant of the car one glance, and instantly turned without the money and ran.

"Hi! stop that fellow!" shouted the man in the car.

"With all my heart," responded Neale O'Neil, joyfully, and, scrambling out of his seat, he gave chase to the lanky man.

The fellow did not keep long to the road, but vaulted a rail fence and started across a muddy field. Neale, protected by his leggings, did not mind the mud, and kept on after the rascal. He had a pretty well defined idea that this fellow who had tried to collect money from Mrs. Heard had merely played constable and was nothing more than a cheap robber. Neale was so angry that he was determined not to let the fellow get away.

He heard the second automobile stop, and supposed the man in it was following, too; but he did not glance back to see. Just then he felt that he could master the lanky man alone, if need be.

And that is exactly what happened. The fellow got to the other side of the field with Neale gaining on him at every jump. Once in the woods there, however, the Milton boy feared the fugitive would be able to hide from him. So Neale increased his pace, sprinting for the last few rods, and caught the fellow just as he reached the fence. Neale tackled low, in true football fashion, and brought the long-legged man down with a crash. There they both rolled on the muddy ground, Neale clinging to the fellow's knees, and the latter clawing and snarling like a wildcat.

Sammy Pinkney had followed the chase as far as the top rail of the roadside fence, where Mrs. Heard had commanded him in no uncertain tone to stop. There the little fellow stood, waving his cap and yelling encouragement to Neale O'Neil, while the stranger from the second automobile strode across the field at a rapid gait.

"Good boy!" shouted this stranger, heartily. "Hang on to him."

Neale hung. His face was scratched and his clothing muddy; but the long-legged fellow could not do him very much harm before help came. Indeed, when he once saw that he was bound to be captured he stopped struggling and began actually to blubber.

"I was only foolin'," he whined. "Lemme up, boy. I wouldn't hurt ye."

"I know you won't hurt me," snapped Neale. "I won't let you—that's why."

"Hold on to him!" shouted the other man again.

Neale let the rascal up; but he hung to his coat-collar with both hands.

"I was just a-foolin'," repeated the captive, and he actually shook with terror. "Ye know, Sheriff, I'm always foolin'."

Neale looked then with increased interest upon the big man who was approaching. This must be Sheriff Keech, Luke Shepard's friend.

"So you got the ornery critter, did you?" demanded the county officer, panting from his exertions. "Good boy."

"Aw, say, now, Sheriff! you know I'm only foolin'," almost wept the captive.

"Oh, I know you're the town cut-up, Abe," growled the sheriff. "But this time you'll have a chance to think it over in jail. Why!" he added, to Neale, "I knew who this must be the minute Luke Shepard told me about him; and as I saw him come down the road about an hour ago, I had a hunch I'd just about catch him at his capers."

"Aw, Sheriff," begged the fellow. "Don't you be too hard on me. I jest found that star——"

"You are a rascal!" snapped the county officer. "You sent off to a mail-order house and bought that bum badge and just couldn't keep from flirting around with it. Showing what you thought you'd do if you was a constable. Oh, I'll put you where the dogs won't bite you."

"I—I never collected no money from 'em," whined the would-be constable.

"No. That's because I came along just a little too soon. I wish you had got the money. Then I would have had you to rights, sure enough," declared the sheriff, bitterly.

"Oh, let him go, young man. He won't run now; for if he does he'll be resisting arrest, and that'll fix him with the judge for sure."

"Why, say, he isn't right in the head, is he?" demanded Neale O'Neil, wonderingly. "Making out to be a constable, and robbing people, and all that?"

"He's one of these half-baked critters you find once in so often that take correspondence school courses to learn to be detectives, and all that sort of mush. Ugh!"

"Abe" was a very forlorn looking creature as he came out to the road. Sammy on the fence waved his cap again and cheered.

"I tell you, Neale, you're some runner," declared the boy, enthusiastically. "What are you going to do—hang him?"

"That horrid child!" exclaimed Agnes. "I never heard of such a bloodthirsty boy before."

But the rest of the party were inclined to feel that the punishment to be meted out to the fellow who had posed as constable could not be too harsh.

Sheriff Keech ordered Abe to get into his car, and seemed to have no fear that the mean-spirited fellow might try to run away again.

"I know Abe," he said to Mrs. Heard, when she suggested this possibility. "He hasn't any more character than a dishrag. He's arrested now, and he knows it. He wouldn't dare run away from me once I've put my hand on him.

"Now, ma'am, tell me all about it."

Mrs. Heard had plenty of help in relating the circumstances surrounding the touring party's two adventures with this Abe. Everybody wanted to tell what he or she thought of the fellow, even to Dot. The latter said, with conviction:

"He is not a nice man at all, and I'm awfully glad he doesn't live anywhere near our house."

"I don't know that any neighborhood would give Abe a bonus for moving into it," chuckled Mr. Keech. "Well! I won't detain you. I can scare him bad enough as it is. And thirty days in jail will do Abe a world of good. I won't keep you folks as witnesses; you've had trouble enough."

So the matter was settled very amicably, and the touring party from Milton hastened on to the Wayside Rose Inn, at Brampton, for breakfast.

"One thing we never thought about," Agnes said to Neale, when they had bidden Sheriff Keech good-bye.

"What's that?"

"Why, about Mr. Collinger's car and that Joe Dawson fellow. My! what mean pcoplc wc do manage to meet."

"And a little while ago you were thinking what good folks we had met," laughed Neale. "But you are mistaken, Aggie. I spoke to the sheriff about Saleratus Joe and his mate and the lost car. Nothing doing. I've asked everybody else we have talked with—the blacksmith and Luke Shepard and all—about that bunch."

"Oh! have you, Neale?" cried Mrs. Heard. "And has nothing come of it?"

"Well, Mrs. Heard," said the boy, "all trace of that car and those fellows seems to have ended right there at the Higgins' farm—where the Gypsy king saw them for the last time. That's the way it looks to me."

"Oh, dear me!" sighed Agnes. "I wish you'd have let me hunt in that barn for the car."

"Or me," put in Sammy, with confidence.

"Say! you two give me a pain," cried Neale, and refused to talk about it any further.

They made a fine run that day, getting on good roads again, and they spent the night with friends of Mrs. Heard's who had been on the lookout for them for two days. A letter was waiting for the chaperone from her nephew, stating that the police were looking for Saleratus Joe and another man in connection with the disappearance of the Maybrouke runabout, and that the information she had sent might aid in the arrest of the automobile thieves.

"Well," said Agnes, "of course I hope the police catch them; but it would be fun if we could bring about their arrest and find the machine, too, Neale."

"Don't let it worry you, Aggie," he advised. "There isn't any reward offered, so you'd have your work for your pains."

Just the same, neither of them forgot the matter, and it was a topic of conversation between them, now and then, throughout the entire tour.

They went on as far as Fort Kritchton, and spent the week-end at the Monolith Hotel there, to which their trunks had been forwarded. The car needed some slight repairs, and the girls found pleasant friends. This point was to be the farthest they expected to travel from Milton.

Neale found a party of boys camping up in the woods above the hotel, and he enjoyed himself, too; but he had to take Sammy along with him most of the time, and he declared to Agnes that if he ever went anywhere again and had his choice of taking Sammy or a flea, he would choose the flea!

"You have no more idea of where to find him from one moment to another than a flea," growled the older boy. "I'm coming to the old bachelor's belief in the treatment and bringing up of boys."

"What is that?" asked the amused Agnes, who had had her own experiences with Sammy Pinkney.

"Why, the crabbed old bachelor, who had six small nephews, declared he believed all boys should be taken at about three years of age and put in barrels, the heads nailed on, and that they should be fed through the bungholes."

"Goodness!" laughed Agnes. "And when they grew up?"

"'Drive in the bungs,'" declared Neale, seriously. "That was his creed and I am about ready to subscribe to it."

Sammy, however, had a good time. He confided to Mrs. Heard and Ruth that he had never had such a good time in his life. He got letters and money from his mother and father, just as the Corner House girls did, likewise, from home; and he was actually growing sturdy looking as well as brown.

"Whether this tour does anybody else good or not, Sammy P. is being helped," declared Mrs. Heard.

"'Sammy P. Buttinsky,'" sniffed Agnes. "Such a plague. I believe his mother will lose ten years of her age in appearance during this time of Sammy's absence. She certainly ought to be our friend for life."

After all, however, they none of them could really be "mad at" Sammy, as Tess said. He was a plague; but there was something really attractive about him, too.

"He is the most un-moral child I ever heard of," Ruth said. "He seems to have stepped right out of the stone age."

Mrs. Heard smiled at that statement. "My dear girl," she said, "most boys are that way. Philly Collinger was—and look at him now," for Mrs. Heard was very proud indeed of the county surveyor. "I think there is one very helpful thing that you Corner House girls are missing."

"What is that, Mrs. Heard?" asked Ruth, in curiosity.

"You have missed having a brother or two. They are great educators for the feminine mind," laughed the lady.

However, Sammy behaved himself pretty well—considering—all the time the touring party remained at the Monolith Hotel. The little girls whom Tess and Dot played with looked somewhat askance at Sammy, for his boasted intention of following in the sanguinary wake of Captain Kidd, Blackbeard, and Sir Henry Morgan, set him as a creature apart from the rest of boykind. In fact, among the little folk, Sammy Pinkney was quite the sensation for several days. Then little Eddie Haflinger developed a carbuncle on the back of his neck and Sammy's swashbuckling tendencies rather paled before the general interest in Eddie's stiff neck.

However, everybody had a good time at Fort Kritchton; but the "call of the wild," as Agnes expressed it, was the stronger. They had had so many adventures—pleasant as well as disconcerting—on the road, that even Mrs. Heard was glad when the time came to leave the resort.

"Let's send our trunks right back to Milton," Agnes said. "No more 'Fluffy Ruffles' for mine till we get home. Let's rough it."

Their bags in the automobile really did contain all they would need, so it was agreed to live in plain and serviceable garments for the rest of the trip.

"If we run short of clean linen and handkerchiefs," said Ruth, "we shall have to stop and do our washing in a brook. How about that?"

"I suppose you'll want to stretch lines over the auto and dry your clothes as we travel," growled Neale O'Neil. "Then if we meet some fidgety old farmer-woman with a more fidgety horse—good-night!"

"I wish," Agnes declared, "that we had brought a tent with us—a nice one like the Shepards have. Wouldn't it have been fun to camp out every night—just like those Gypsies?"

"How about it when it rained?" asked Ruth.

"Well, we've been out in one rainstorm—and we're neither sugar nor salt," said her sister, sticking to her guns.

"But never again—if I can help it," cried Mrs. Heard. "It is all right for you young folks; but my blood is not so young as yours; nor is my appetite for adventure and what you call 'fun' quite so keen as it used to be."

It was a fact. The young folks only laughed at that memorable experience when they were overtaken by the storm. It was all what Agnes called "fun."

The touring party planned a roundabout way home to Milton, in order to see a part of the country that they had not before driven through.

"And we'll take the good roads, too. I understand more about this map and guide book than I did," proclaimed Neale O'Neil.

However, at one point they agreed to leave the better traveled roads so as to spend another night with the crossroads blacksmith and "Mother." And they half hoped to meet the Shepards near there, also.

"That'll bring us around past the Higgins farm, too," Neale said, thoughtfully.

"Oh, Neale! I want to take a look into that barn myself," cried Agnes.

"Pshaw!" responded her boy friend. "If that car of Mr. Collinger's was ever there, Saleratus Joe and his chum have got it away long since, of course."

But Agnes was hopeful. She usually was of a sanguine mind.

CHAPTER XXI—THE UNEXPECTED HAPPENS

The automobile party did not travel all day long—whirling over the dusty roads, past flower-spangled fields, or through pleasant woods. No, indeed.

Little folks especially—like Tess and Dot and Sammy—cannot sit patiently, even in an upholstered touring car, hour after hour. It was pleasant to ride so smoothly through the lovely country; it was nicer still to halt by the wayside and hunt for adventure.

Tom Jonah, who was by nature a tramp, enjoyed the excursions away from the automobile as much as did the children—and he was never again off their trail at such times. If Tess and Dot and Sammy left the party, somebody would be sure to speak to the old dog, and up he would get in order to follow the children. He had not forgotten the occasion when the two smallest Corner House girls had escaped his watchful eye. So Tom Jonah was what the slangy Sammy Pinkney called "Johnny on the Spot" one day when something quite exciting happened.

They had stopped beside the road for lunch, as they almost always did, and as soon as they had eaten the children were anxious to explore.

The almost dry bed of a water-course attracted their attention, and as they could step from rock to rock, and so keep their feet dry, they started up this ravine. Sammy, of course, led and recklessly leaped from rock to rock with the assurance of a goat. The little girls were agile enough; but Tess gave much attention to Dot, and the latter had to be sure that the Alice-doll got into no difficulty.

"You mustn't go so fast, Sammy," urged Tess. "You know we haven't got to catch a train. And do go away, Tom Jonah! You're all wet. When you shake yourself I'd just as lief be walking close behind a sprinkling-cart."

Both the boy and the dog laughed at her; but Dot, realizing that Alice's best gown might be ruined, almost fell off her stepping-stone as Tom Jonah deliberately shook himself again and she tried to shield her doll's finery.

"Oh, bully!" shouted Sammy, suddenly. "There's blackberries."

The bushes were overhanging the steep wall of the ravine on one side. Tess looked doubtfully up the rocky slope.

"They're mostly red, Sammy," she objected. "Or green."

"Some of 'em's black enough," declared the boy. "Come on! Let's get some."

Sammy scrambled up the rough side of the gully. Tom Jonah bounded after him and then looked back at his little mistresses to see if they were coming too.

"Well! I won't be beaten by a boy," said Tess, with sudden decision. "Let's go too, Dot."

It was a rather hard pull for the little girls; and Dot got her knees "scrubby," although she saved the Alice-doll's dress. They came to the top of the height all but breathless and with flushed faces.

Sammy was coolly picking the best berries and cramming them into a mouth which betrayed to all who might behold his greediness. "You better hurry up," he advised, with a lofty detachment from all chivalry, "or there won't be any left. There ain't many ripe ones, after all."

"Well, I do declare!" exclaimed Tess. "You aren't very polite, Sammy Pinkney."

"You—you might have saved us some!" protested Dot.

The little girls looked all about. They did not see any other blackberry bushes in the vicinity. But Tess sighted something else.

"Oh, Dot! Roses! Lovely, pink, wild, roses! Did you ever see so many?"

There was a veritable hedge of the pretty, fragrant, delicate flowers at the far side of this little field. The two girls raced over to them at once, forgetting both Sammy's greediness and the berries. Tom Jonah bounded after them, and rushed through a gap in the rose hedge. Instantly there was excitement on the far side of the hedge, just out of sight.

An angry and excited voice rose in a familiar: "Bla-a-a-t! bla-a-a-t!"

"Oh, my! what's that?" asked Dot, startled.

"It sounds just like Billy Bumps," said Tess.

Again it sounded: "Ba-a-a! bla-a-a-t!" Tom Jonah barked. Sammy came running over to them.

"Hear that old Billy goat?" he shouted. "I bet Tom Jonah's treed him!"

He dived through the break in the hedge and perforce, because of their curiosity, the little Corner House girls were drawn after him. There they found both Tom Jonah and the boy dancing about a rather savage-looking black-faced ram that had been tied to a stump and that was now so wound up in his rope that he could do little but stamp his hoofs and shake his horns at his tormentors.

"Oh, Sammy! don't worry the poor goat," begged Dot.

"Come here, Tom Jonah!" commanded Tess sternly, and the dog obeyed if the boy did not.

"Aw, what's the odds? He can't get at us," said Sammy, careless of both his grammar and the ethics of the case. "And he's only an old goat."

"That is just horrid of you, Sammy Pinkney!" declared Tess. "Suppose it was our own poor Billy Bumps?"

The girls, no more than the boy, did not recognize the difference between the goat they knew well and the ram that they had never seen before. The black-faced rogue had been tied because it was not safe to let him run loose with the herd.

"We must help him," declared Tess, having made Tom Jonah go to the rear. "We can't leave him tied here to suffer—and all wound up in that rope. If Neale were only here——"

"Oh, yes!" agreed Dot. "Neale would fix it all right."

"Say," declared Sammy, spurred to the quick, "I ain't afraid. If Neale could do it, I guess I can. But just the same, I bet if we let him loose he'll chase us."

"Oh, no! he wouldn't do that, would he?" cried Dot.

"He wouldn't be so ungrateful," said Tess severely.

"Poor, poor old Billy," cooed Dot, putting out her hand to the ram.

"He—he doesn't look just like our goat; but I know he's suffering," Tess declared.

The noise the ram made would naturally lead one to think that he was suffering. If not urged on by this appearance, Sammy desired to make a certain impression upon his companions. He walked boldly up to the stump to which the ram was tethered. Things began to happen immediately! That black-faced ram had no more idea of gratitude than a rattlesnake.

Sammy got two loops of the rope off the stump, and another off the ram's hind leg. The beast immediately put down its head and bumped Sammy just as hard as he possibly could.

"Ow! Ouch!" yelled Sammy. "Get out, you mean thing!"

"Bla-a-at!" said the ram, and tried to charge again. Sammy attempted to scramble out of the way; the little girls screamed; Tom Jonah began to bark and to jump about the excited party.

The ram ran several times around the stump in the right direction to unwind his rope; but in so doing he got Sammy and the rope entangled. In a moment more the modern pirate was lashed to the post, yelling vigorously, while the ram was brought to a stop again on too short a rope to do the boy any damage with his ugly horns, although he threatened Sammy continuously.

The screams of the three children and the barking of Tom Jonah was bound to raise the neighborhood. A shout soon replied, and the screaming of other youthful voices. Into the field at its far end came a man, running, and close upon his heels several ragged and bare-legged children, both boys and girls.

"What are ye doin' there, ye little imps?" roared the man, bearing down on the little Corner House girls and their unfortunate champion in a very ugly way.

"Oh, do help Sammy!" begged Tess, with clasped hands, of the ugly man.

Dot, hugging the Alice-doll closely, stared wonderingly at the horde of little ragamuffins that came dancing and screeching to the scene of Sammy's disaster.

"Take him off, mister, an' lemme get away," cried Sammy. "I won't never do it again."

It was so natural for Sammy Pinkney to be blamed in whatever situation he found himself, that he offered his apologies at once. The ugly man scowled down at him.

"I'd oughter let old Dewey lam' you good," he growled.

"Cut the rope and let old Dewey go for 'em, Uncle Jim!" yelled one of the young savages.

At that both Tess and Dot burst into despairing wails. At the same moment Neale O'Neil and Agnes burst through the bushes, having been drawn to the spot by the uproar.

"Oh, Aggie!" shrieked Tess.

"Oh, Neale!" cried Dot.

Sammy pluckily held his tongue; but the way he looked at the bigger boy belonging to the automobile party would have touched a much stonier heart than that of Neale O'Neil.

"Keep away from here," commanded the ugly man, to Neale.

"I guess not," responded the boy sharply. "You don't seem to be doing anything to help him."

"What did he want to get tangled up with the ram for, then?" demanded the fellow.

"He was trying to help the poor Billy goat," Tess sobbed, from the shelter of Agnes' arms.

"You city folks are too fresh, anyhow," cried one of the ragged children. "We ought to stone you kids. Hadn't we, Uncle Jim?"

But the man was busy with Neale. "Let that rope alone!" he commanded, as the boy approached the entangled Sammy.

"Stand out of my way," said Neale, taking out his pocketknife and opening the big blade. "And run your old sheep out of here when I cut him free."

"Don't you do that!" cried the man.

But with one stroke of the sharp blade Neale freed both the ram and Sammy.

"Ba-a-a! Bla-a-a-t!" uttered the ram, and shook his horns threateningly at Neale.

"Butt him, Dewey!" yelled the ragamuffins.

But Neale delivered a hearty kick that resounded upon the ram's ribs. With another blat the beast switched around, lowered his head, and charged directly at the ugly man.

"Git out, ye derned nuisance!" yelled the fellow, and only by leaping high and spreading wide his legs did he escape the ram's furious charge.

Missing his object, the ram kept on across the field and, whooping, the rag-and-bobtail crew strung along after him. The man remained to bluster and threaten Neale for a while; but the boy from Milton paid very little attention to him.

"Let's go! Let's go!" Agnes kept saying, and the little girls, thoroughly frightened, kept urging the same thing.

But when they got down into the ravine again, and the ugly man was out of sight, Agnes sent the trio of little folks ahead, and said to Neale:

"Do you know, Neale, who that horrid man was?"

"Huh?" grunted Neale, puzzled.

"Didn't you see who he was when he stood right there before you?"

"Er—'Hawkshaw, the detective'!" scoffed Neale, grinning widely.

"Don't try to be funny," implored Agnes. "Where were your eyes? That was the man we saw the last time with Saleratus Joe, when they passed us in that strange automobile," declared the girl earnestly.

"No?" gasped Neale.

"Yes, it was. I could never forget his ugly face. He is the very man, I believe, who helped Joe steal Mr. Collinger's car."

Neale wagged his head. "Whether he is one of the thieves or not, he's a bad man all right. You can see that," the boy agreed. "I wonder if we ought to hunt up Sheriff Keech?" But they were a long way from the residence of the sheriff whose acquaintance they had previously made.

That night the touring party stopped with the blacksmith and his wife. The Shepards had not returned to this neighborhood, and the Corner House party did not wish to waste any time. They were to make a long detour from this point before going back to Milton. They desired to see a part of the country altogether strange to them.

"Shall we go around by the Higgins farm again?"

That was the query Neale O'Neil propounded before bedtime that evening after they had eaten another of "Mother's" wonderful suppers.

"I don't really see the use," Mrs. Heard said. "I haven't heard a word from Philly Collinger about it. And I told him everything that Gypsy told you, Neale."

"And how Neale hunted in the barn and found no trace of Mr. Collinger's car?" suggested Ruth.

"Oh, yes."

"But he did find something!" cried Agnes.

"What did he find, I'd like to know?" asked her sister.

"He saw where the auto wheels had skidded on the path going up to the barn—didn't you, Neale?"

"Yes," the boy agreed. "But the car wasn't there."

"Pooh! you didn't find it," said the girl scornfully.

"My goodness, Aggie!" cried Ruth, "when you set out to be, you can be the most stubborn person!"

"Oh, well," Mrs. Heard said soothingly, "what if we do go around by that barn and satisfy Agnes? It won't be much out of our way."

It was over a good bit of rough road, however, and that rough road brought calamity to the Corner House car. Neale O'Neil knew something was wrong before they had climbed the long hill to the level of the Higgins farm.

"What's that thumping noise, Neale?" asked the sharp-eared Agnes, who had chosen to ride with the young chauffeur and Sammy and Tom Jonah in the front of the machine.

Neale was scowling. "Ask me an easier one," he growled. "I'm no soothsayer."

"Well! you needn't be so pie-crusty," she said. "Is the car falling to pieces?"

"Maybe."

"Why don't you stop and find out?"

"On this hill? Not much!" declared the boy, his brow still wrinkled with anxiety.

"Well! It's—go-ing—to—stop!" jerked out the prophetic Agnes, as the wheels of the rumbling car seemed to turn more and more slowly.

"What is the matter?" demanded Ruth, from the tonneau. "Is the car stopping?"

Neale manipulated the levers, and the engine roared spitefully; but the speed did not increase, and that sepulchral thumping under the car continued.

"I hope you haven't run out of gasoline again, Neale?" suggested Mrs. Heard.

Neale grunted. Agnes giggled. "My! you could bite nails, couldn't you?" she whispered.

It was most exasperating—no mistake about it! The machine had acted so well all along, that perhaps he had grown careless. Yet Neale could not imagine what it was that had happened now. And away out here in the wilderness! He was sure that rumbling and thumping spelled trouble.

"Don't you mean to stop?" gasped Ruth.

"Not here, I tell you," snapped the exasperated youth. "You want us to get stalled here out of sight of a house, even?"

"We won't be in sight of many houses when we get to the top of the hill, if I remember rightly," murmured Agnes.

Neale made no further reply. The thing continued to thump and the engine to roar. But they reached the top of the hill and continued staggering along toward the farm buildings, which looked as deserted as they had on the previous occasion when the party had stopped here.

"How near are we to a repair garage?" asked Mrs. Heard.

"About twenty miles," Agnes told her. "Sweet prospect, isn't it?"

"But what is the matter?" repeated Ruth.

"If you ask me," said Agnes, with conviction, "I think the old thing has the epizootic."

"Oh, my!" gasped Dot. "That's what the stableman's horse had—and it died. Could our automobile have the same sickness?"

"I don't know; but it acts as if it were going to die," growled Neale.

"Shall—shall we get out and walk?" asked Tess. "Maybe it can't carry so many now."

"Hear the kid!" scoffed Sammy. "'Tain't nothing but an old mess of iron-work. It can't get sick."

There certainly was something, however, seriously the matter with the Corner House girls' automobile. Just as they came abreast of the drive that led up to the big hay barn the engine coughed two or three times, and then stopped dead.

"All out!" ejaculated Neale, in disgust. "This looks like the end of our day's journey."

"And not a house in sight," murmured Mrs. Heard.

CHAPTER XXII—SAMMY INVESTIGATES

It was a lovely afternoon, and there were still two or three hours before sunset. The intention had been merely to stop at the abandoned Higgins farm to satisfy Agnes' desire to make another search of the premises for the lost motor car.

"I believe you wanted to look down the well to see if it was there," Neale remarked, grumpily. "Well! you've time enough to do it."

"Oh, Neale! don't be nasty," said his girl chum. "I'm sorry if the old car is going to make you trouble——"

"Us trouble, I should say," Ruth said, rather sharply. "Do you realize that we are an unconscionable long way from civilization?"

"Well, don't let us become savage, if the wilderness is," said Mrs. Heard, recovering her own good temper. "Of course, Neale, you don't know just what the matter is with the machine?"

"Not yet; but I'm going to find out," he returned, hauling his overalls and jumper out of the tool-box.

"And us," cried Dot. "Let's look around for the place where we're going to camp. Why! we'll be just like the Gypsies again."

"My goodness!" groaned Mrs. Heard. "That child is uncanny. Does she know that we are going to be marooned here all night? And not a soul in sight!"

"We got something to eat," said Sammy, who had investigated. "I'll get the fire ready to light. Neale won't let me have matches."

"I'm sure we could clean out one of those small houses, and make it nice and comfortable for us to live in," said Tess, falling in with the idea with enthusiasm.

"Me for the hay!" cried Agnes, running up to the barn door. "We'll sleep in the hay!"

"Remember the rats!" hissed Neale, as he crept under the car with a hammer and a collection of wrenches.

"Mean thing!" cried Agnes. "I won't believe there are such things, so now!"

When she opened the small barn door, however, she had a fright right at the start. Something whisked out at her feet, and Agnes leaped aside with a scream.

"Oh! it's a pussy-cat," cried Dot delightedly. "Then somebody does live here!"

It was a beautiful blue Maltese cat, and although she was a little wild at first, she must have been used to children when the farmer lived here, for Dot and Tess soon coaxed her to come to be petted.

"Anyway," Agnes said, "I'm not going to worry about rats with a fine puss like her around. She can handle the rats."

"Sure. She eats 'em alive," called Neale from beneath the car.

Agnes went inside and struggled with the bar of the big barn door. Sammy finally went to her assistance and they swung the doors open so that the sunlight might flood the interior. Nothing seemed to be changed since Neale had made his search more than two weeks before.

Mrs. Heard and Ruth were wandering about the premises, looking into the other outbuildings. The stable was empty, of course. There was no stock on the place. But on the other side of the ruins of the burned dwelling they made quite an important discovery.

There was a fenced-in garden patch. It was weed-grown for the most part; but there were berry bushes loaded with dew-berries and raspberries, both black and red; besides ripening gooseberries and currants. Here was a feast for the children, and Ruth was about to call them when Mrs. Heard said:

"Wait. If we should have to remain to-night, this fruit will help out for supper and breakfast. We have plenty of sugar and canned evaporated milk."

"Goodness me, Mrs. Heard! Don't talk so perfectly recklessly!" Ruth exclaimed. "It can't be that we shall have to remain here. Why, we can't!"

"What are you going to do—walk to the next town?" asked Agnes, who came to them in time to overhear this statement of her sister's.

"Where is the next town?" asked Mrs. Heard quickly.

"Just sixteen miles away by the map—and fourteen at least as the crow flies," Agnes said promptly.

"And we're not crows," murmured Ruth.

"We can never walk fourteen miles—or more," Mrs. Heard said, with conviction. "Where is the nearest house?"

"Goodness only knows. There is no other farm on this road—we know that. And I don't remember seeing any very near to where we turned into it at either end, do you?" said Agnes.

"No, I don't," Ruth admitted, shaking her head. "We are in a fix if Neale can't repair the car himself—and quickly."

"Don't say anything to him," begged Agnes. "He's as cross as a bear with a sore head."

Meanwhile Mrs. Heard and the two girls were approaching the automobile.

"Ouch!" grunted Neale from under the car, and Agnes giggled.

"Now he's bumped his poor head again, and it's sorer than ever."

They waited for the final verdict—Mrs. Heard in a serious mind if the girls were not. Finally Neale backed out from beneath the machine. He held a casting in his hand, and it was so badly cracked that, when he pressed the halves apart, it broke in two pieces.

"There's the blamed thing!" he pronounced, with scowling emphasis.

"Sh!" exclaimed Ruth. "Don't use such language. Can't it be fixed?"

"Oh, yes. They grow these things on bushes right out yonder in the fields. All I've got to do is to go and pick one that fits this breed of car. Oh, yes!" retorted Neale O'Neil.

"It is tragic!" gasped Mrs. Heard.

"Then we surely will have to stay here to-night," said Agnes, and she did not sound as though the prospect worried her much.

"And to-morrow night—and the next night—and for several more, if you ask me," growled Neale. "That is, unless I can get a wagon and drive you all to the nearest railroad station, and send you back to Milton."

"Nev-air!" cried Agnes. "Let you stay here and have all the fun? Stingy!"

"My goodness, child," murmured the chaperone. "What do you call fun?"

"At least, it would be a novel experience," Ruth admitted.

"You, too?" gasped Mrs. Heard. "I thought you had better sense, Ruth Kenway."

"Well—I haven't," admitted the oldest Corner House girl, smiling. "How are you going to get the thing repaired, Neale?"

"Wire to the makers. Take two or three days to get the new casting. And we can't run a yard without it."

"Where will you send your telegram from?" Ruth asked.

"From the flag station—Hickton—and that's seven miles away. I'll have to walk it unless I find some one to drive me there."

"Oh, Neale! To-night?" cried Agnes.

"No. Couldn't get to the station before it was closed, anyway. I'll make an early start. That is, unless you want me to hike right out now and find a farmer who will cart you all to some place where you can get regular beds."

"Oh, no!" cried Agnes, again. "You sha'n't have all the fun, Neale."

"No-o, Neale," said Ruth, more slowly. "I think it will be possible for us all to stay here with you. The weather is so nice."

"Oh, let's stay! Let's stay!" cried the three juveniles in chorus, and even Tom Jonah, becoming excited too, barked his approval.

"Well, what can I do," Mrs. Heard demanded, "with every one against me?"

So it was agreed to stay. First of all, Neale declared the car must be got into the barn, for it might rain; and then, it did not look well to have the automobile standing out in the open road.

"I'd like to know who you suppose is going to see it here?" demanded Agnes, with a sniff. "I don't believe anybody ever drives through this road more than once a month—or unless there is a funeral in the family!"

"Maybe Saleratus Joe and that other fellow will be driving through in Mr. Collinger's runabout," said Neale slyly.

"Oh, if they only would!" gasped Agnes.

"A fat chance!" returned Neale. "And what if they did? Would you hold 'em up the way that imitation constable did us, and take the car away from them?"

"I don't know what I'd do," said Agnes. "But I'd do something."

Meanwhile the boy rummaged around in the barn and found a set of blocks and the necessary tackle. This he rigged to a beam inside the barn and carried the rope to the car at the foot of the sloping driveway.

With the purchase this arrangement gave them, the young folks all "tailed" on to the rope like sailors and managed to drag the automobile into the barn; but they were more than an hour and a half at the work, and it was growing dark when they finished.

Meanwhile nobody had appeared to forbid their camping on the Higgins premises. A fire had been built in the open and the tripod set up. Mrs. Heard tucked up her skirts and grilled bacon (and her face) at the fire. There were eggs, too, and canned tongue and biscuits and plenty of fruit. They all thought it great fun.

After supper, as it was still too early for bed, the three children entered into a boisterous game of hide-and-go-seek. Sammy, burrowing in the great heap of hay at the rear of the barn floor, suddenly lost his interest in the game. He dragged something out of the hay and brought it to Neale, who sat on the sill of the big door with pad and pencil, composing the telegram he intended to send to the automobile manufacturers from Hickton the next morning.

"What's that you have, Sammy P.?" demanded Agnes, as the little fellow, too excited to speak, put the object in Neale's hands.

"Great cracky!" ejaculated Neale O'Neil. "Where did you get it?"

"Under the hay. There's something there. I broke the wire that held it—see?" said Sammy, excitedly.

"A license plate!" gasped Agnes.

"State license number! What do you know about that? Ask Mrs. Heard——"

Agnes was away like the wind. Mrs. Heard and Ruth were washing dishes at the horse trough. The girl brought the chaperone in a hurry.

"What was Mr. Collinger's license number, do you know?" Neale asked her. "I mean his automobile license number."

"The license number is twenty-four hundred and thirty-two. Goodness! I ought to remember it."

Neale stood up with the license plate in his hand. "We've found the car, sure as you live!" he said, with conviction.

CHAPTER XXIII—ROUGHING IT

Agnes had an excellent opportunity to say "I told you so!" to Neale; but did not even mention to her boy chum the fact that he could not have searched the barn very thoroughly upon his first visit to the place.

For Mr. Collinger's stolen automobile was there under the hay. By the light of their own automobile lanterns Neale uncovered the runabout and finally hauled it out on the barn floor.

"What do you suppose is the matter with it?" asked Ruth.

"Why, nothing, of course," cried Mrs. Heard, almost in tears, she was so happy. "Philly will be so delighted."

"Guess I'd better telegraph to him in the morning when I send for that casting—eh?" said Neale.

"Oh! if you will, Neale," said the chaperone. "He can come and get the car himself. Oh, dear me! isn't this just the finest thing that's happened to us during our tour?"

"It is, indeed, Mrs. Heard," Ruth agreed.

"And all because of Sammy," said Neale. "Sammy, you're some kid."

"Of course I am," agreed that irrepressible. "I guess you're all glad now that I came with you, ain't you?"

There was nothing bashful about Sammy Pinkney. He demanded and received all the credit due him.

Nor did Agnes and Neale begrudge him the honor—and certainly not Mrs. Heard. The discovery of the stolen car was sufficient to make Mrs. Heard forget their present discomforts; while Neale and Agnes felt that their suspicions of Saleratus Joe and the ugly man had been proved true.

"The Gypsy king told us the exact truth," Agnes said. "I thought he was an honest man."

"Of course," Dot said wonderingly. "Wasn't he a king, even if he didn't wear a crown and carry a scalper?"

"And won't Philly Collinger be glad? Won't he be glad?" Mrs. Heard cried, over and over again.

Meanwhile Neale was going carefully over the recovered runabout; but he could not examine it thoroughly by lantern-light.

"Of course, it broke down or something," he said. "Or they wouldn't have abandoned it here. Just as soon as the farmer came for some of his hay he'd have found the car. Saleratus Joe couldn't have intended to leave it here for long unless it needed repairing. That is, it doesn't seem as if he would."

"He may come back here—he and the ugly man—any time!" whispered Agnes in his ear.

"Sh! nonsense!" commanded Neale. "Anyway, we have Tom Jonah. I'll give the car a thorough going over when I come back from the railroad to-morrow."

The excitement occasioned by Sammy's discovery kept them all awake longer than usual. Besides, camping out in this way had not become familiar enough to the party for them to have become used to it. Only on the night they had remained with Luke and Cecile Shepard had they experienced anything at all like this present situation.

It was agreed by all that they should bed in the hay. With robes and dust-cloths from their car they made themselves very comfortable in the heaped-up, fragrant mass of dried grass at the back of the barn.

"We are 'bedding down' just like cattle," giggled Agnes. "Isn't it fun?"

It was very comfortable, whether it was fun or not, and they soon went to sleep and slept as heavily as the seven sleepers—whoever they may have been—until daybreak. Tom Jonah lay at the open barn door and kept faithful watch.

Neale was astir first, and he built a fire and made coffee. Agnes smelled the coffee, and soon ran out in her stocking feet with her shoes in her hand.

"Oh, Neale!" she whispered shrilly. "This is the life! Isn't it just great? I could live this way always. Where do you wash?"

"At the horse-trough," said the boy.

"Oh-o! I don't like that," she objected.

"Dear me!" responded Neale, in a shrill falsetto, and grinning at her. "And you could live this way always!"

"Mean thing!" she retorted. "Folks can be nice if they do live like Gypsies."

"Or hoboes," added the boy.

"Well——"

"Pump fresh water for yourself, of course," said Neale. "And put on your shoes or you'll bruise your feet on these pebbles."

"My, yes! I feel as if I were doing penance," confessed Agnes, hastening to pull on her shoes.

They had a cozy time drinking the hot coffee and munching crackers before the others were even astir.

"I'll bring back a lot of grub," promised Neale.

"And a tube of cold-cream; Ruth and I are all out. And a bottle of witch hazel, and some animal crackers, because the kids like 'em. And some hand lotion for Mrs. Heard—I know her bottle is almost empty. And do get good tea. And don't forget the stuffed olives——"

"Hold on," interposed Neale, beginning to count on his fingers. "Let's see if I can remember all those. First, a tub of cold cream——"

"Tube! tube!" cried Agnes.

"Oh! Ah! There is a difference, isn't there?" he responded, grinning, and named the other articles over with some exactness. "All right. If my memory—and my money—doesn't give out I'll bring them all, even if I have to hire a four-horse wagon to cart the stuff."

He started away at once, and was out of sight before the rest of the party appeared from the barn, yawning but deliciously rested. Sweet-smelling hay for a bed cannot be improved upon.

"Only," Tess observed, "I don't feel just right because I haven't been all undressed. Don't you s'pose, Ruthie, that we could take turns having a bath in the horse-trough?"

The others laughed at her; and it was agreed that it was not going to be much of a cross, after all, to remain on the abandoned farm for the few days it would be necessary to wait for the new part for the automobile.

Neale O'Neil was two hours in getting to Hickton, for it was a long seven miles and the roads were sandy. And along the way he did not pass a dozen houses, and none of them was very near to the Higgins farm. Still, it was not later than eight o'clock when he sent the telegram to the automobile factory, which was not very far away; and he ordered the new casting sent C. O. D. to the Hickton station.

Then he telegraphed to Mr. Collinger, at Milton, in Mrs. Heard's name. The surveyor's aunt had written her message carefully, so that the ordinary reader would not understand just where the stolen car was. Mr. Collinger was to come to Hickton and there inquire for the party of motor car tourists.

There were two stores in sight of the railway station, and in them Neale managed to buy enough food to last his party several days, including eggs and milk and country butter and cheese.

Neale could never have carried all these things back to the farm, but he found a long-legged boy with a rattling wagon drawn by a pony, and bargained with the youth for transportation to the Higgins farm. When the boy learned that a touring party was camped at the site of the burned farmhouse, he was greatly amused.

"Guess old man Higgins don't know about it, does he?" the lad asked.

"I don't suppose he does," admitted Neale. "But we are not doing any harm there."

"He, he! I reckon yer critters won't eat up his hay, that's sure."

"No. Our motive power feeds on gasoline," Neale laughed.

"By jinks! I s'pose that's so. But I'll drive around to old man Higgins and tell him yer camping there—jest ter see what he'll say."

Neale told Mrs. Heard this, and the chaperone decided to send a note to the owner of the place, requesting permission to remain at the abandoned farm and offering to pay for the accommodation if the owner so desired.

The party was quite settled in the camping place by this time.

"We really are Gypsies," Mrs. Heard said. "And I never in my life saw children so delighted as these of ours are at the present time. Goodness! they will never want to live properly again."

It was not alone the little folks who fully enjoyed the situation. Ruth found a big, clean galvanized iron pail and proceeded to wash all the clothes that did not need starch and a hot iron. She had filled a long line before Neale returned from Hickton.

After the noon meal Neale went to work on the stolen car. He made an important discovery in a very short time. There was absolutely nothing the matter with Mr. Collinger's car, though there was no gasoline in the tank!

"I wonder if those fellows found it out before they abandoned it here?" Mrs. Heard queried.

"Well, if they went away just to get some gas for it, they've been gone a long time," giggled Agnes. "But Neale might have saved himself the walk to Hickton if he'd found this out last night."

"Oh, yes; if the rabbit hadn't stopped to take a nap he'd have won the race over Mr. Tortoise," retorted Neale. "We know all about those might-have-beens."

"But—really—I wonder," said the chaperone slowly.

"You wonder what, Mrs. Heard?" asked Ruth.

"I wonder what became of those maps and things that Philly was so careful of. If they were in the car——"

"Then Saleratus Joe got 'em," said Neale promptly.

"No. I don't believe the politicians who instigated the robbery have obtained what they hoped to find in this car. I—wonder—where—they—are."

"Not in the gasoline tank, that's sure," said Neale. "I looked in it."

They all laughed at that, and Mrs. Heard abandoned the puzzling subject.

There was nothing to do of importance but to wait for the message from the automobile factory. Neale tried out the car that had been stolen from Mrs.

Heard's nephew and Mrs. Heard herself enjoyed a ride in it. It was a very good car indeed, and beautifully upholstered.

"I know Philly told me he had this car built according to his own plans, and I've wondered since if he didn't have a place built in it in which to hide his private papers," Mrs. Heard said. "It would be just like him."

"Oh! wouldn't that be great?" cried Agnes.

"And then maybe the maps and things are in the car," Ruth said.

"Who knows? I am quite confident, because of what my nephew said, that the bundle the thieves got in the car was worthless. I remember his saying: 'Those rascals won't get what they want unless they tear my car to pieces.' Now, what could he have meant by that?"

The problem interested the older Corner House girls and Neale very much. Agnes examined the upholstering and the panel-work of the runabout very closely.

"Perhaps Saleratus Joe did find the papers. That's why the car was abandoned here," she said to Neale, with a sigh.

"Well, if they found the secret panel," said the boy, grinning, "they didn't leave it open so we could find it, did they?"

"You needn't make fun," said Agnes. "If I find the papers I won't tell you—so now!"

"Help yourself," he returned. "I'm not half so much interested in Mr. Collinger's affairs as I am in our own car. I hope the factory hustles that casting right along."

They could not expect it yet, and the remainder of the day was spent in roaming about the farm. The children found the biggest huckleberry pasture any of them had ever seen. Mrs. Heard's housewifely desires were spurred.

"I do wish these berries were near Milton," she declared. "I'd can enough of them to last the winter through for huckleberry pies."

They were getting supper, Gypsy fashion, when the lanky boy with the pony drove up with the answers to the telegrams Neale had sent that morning from the Hickton station.

"Hurrah!" shouted Neale, the moment he read his message. "The thing is already shipped. When does the first train from the south stop at Hickton in the morning?" he asked the messenger.

"Eight-thirty," was the reply.

"It will be on that. I'll run over in Mr. Collinger's car and get it."

"And Philly says he'll come up here some time to-morrow, too," announced Mrs. Heard. "We sha'n't have to live in a barn but one night more."

"Oh, say!" drawled the country lad. "Old man Higgins says you kin stay here as long as ye want to, if ye don't burn up the rest o' the buildings."

CHAPTER XXIV—SOMETHING REALLY EXCITING

A very red-faced sun awoke the touring party the next morning, his first rays shooting directly into the broad doorway of the barn—an intruder that Tom Jonah, faithful watchman as he was, could not keep out. The sunshine shone directly into the eyes of the Corner House girls and their friends.

All were quickly astir. They expected to be on their way again before night; and although roughing it had been fun, there were some drawbacks to it.

"We'll sleep in regular beds again to-night," Agnes said, with some satisfaction.

"But I don't believe it will be half so nice," Tess observed. "This hay is so sweet and smelly."

"Now, Sammy Pinkney!" cried Dot, suddenly spying that youngster in mischief, "don't pull that nice pussy's tail. It hurts her."

"Ain't pulling her tail," replied Sammy promptly. "I'm only holding her tail. The cat's doing all the pulling."

Agnes bore down upon him and he immediately ceased holding poor pussy's tail.

"Say! you're awful particular," complained the boy. "I wasn't really hurting the old cat, Aggie. And—and it ain't polite to always be interferin' with a feller."

"Now you've got it, Aggie," chuckled Neale O'Neil. "You see you're not polite. And politeness costs nothing."

"Oh! doesn't it?" returned Agnes. "Suppose you'd put 'very respectfully yours' at the end of that telegram you sent to the auto factory? I guess you'd have found it cost something."

"Stung again!" admitted Neale.

"Why, what is all this I hear?" demanded Ruth, coming up from the horse trough pump bearing a brimming pail of water. "Did somebody get out of bed on the wrong side this bright and beautiful morning?"

"It was the cat," said Neale, in a sepulchral voice. "She started it."

"Which side is the wrong side of a hay-mow bed, Ruthie?" Tess asked.

"That's a poser," Neale said. "You'll have to ask somebody else about that, eh, Ruth? Now, hustle along the breakfast, you girls, for I must start for Hickton."

"And I'm going with you, Neale," Agnes declared. "You can speed up that runabout as fast as you want to. The others won't be along to object."

This last remark she whispered in Neale's ear.

"I tell you, Aggie, you're a speed maniac," responded Neale. "But if Mrs. Heard says you may go off alone with me, all right."

Agnes had learned by this time to wheedle the good-natured chaperone into agreeing to almost anything the girls desired; and of course she had no objection to Agnes' going anywhere with Neale. Whether the Corner House girls realized it or not, they could not have had a brother any more careful for them or better to them than Neale O'Neil.

So the girl and boy chums were on the road in the runabout soon after eight. Mr. Collinger's was a good machine, and it ran smoothly. But Agnes suddenly had an unhappy thought.

"Oh, Neale!" she said, clasping her hands.

"Shoot!" advised the boy, with his eyes on the road ahead.

"We're riding in a stolen car."

"Sure we are. What of it?"

"And all the constables and sheriffs and policemen all over the State have the description of this car and her license number. What are you going to do if an officer holds us up?"

"Cracky! never thought of it," admitted the boy. "I expect they'll jail us."

"Horrid thing! But we may have an unpleasant time explaining it."

"Well, let us hope nothing like that occurs," he said; but Agnes was troubled by the possibility of arrest all the way to the station and back again.

The casting was waiting for them and Neale paid the expressman and then the runabout was headed for the Higgins farm. As Neale and Agnes came in view of the farm buildings none of their party was in sight; but coming across a distant field were two men who seemed to be carrying something heavy between them.

"First natives we've seen wandering around here," Neale observed. "And where are the folks?"

"All gone berrying," Agnes replied. "They said they were going to fill every receptacle we have before leaving the Higgins place. I never did see so many berries."

Neale ran the runabout up to the barn, but did not drive it inside. The big doors had been closed and their own car stood within on the barn floor, but out of sight.

"Let's go berrying too, just as soon as I slip this thing into place," Neale suggested.

Although the broken casting had caused so much trouble, it did not take five minutes to put the new one into place. He tried the engine, and everything worked well.

"All right," he announced, coming out of the small door of the barn again. "Shall we chase over after the others?"

"Yes. And tell them it's all right. We can start off any time now," Agnes said.

"Hullo! I guess we'll have to wait for Mr. Collinger to show up for his car."

"Oh, dear me, yes. I did not think of that," Agnes returned. "I—I wish Mrs. Heard hadn't telegraphed for him. Then we could have driven his car to Milton with ours too. I could have driven it."

"No license, Aggie," said Neale. "You can't drive a car. Say! did you see that?"

"See what, Neale?" she asked him, looking all around.

"I thought I saw a man slip behind that far shed."

"Why! what's become of those two men we saw crossing the field yonder?" demanded the girl, with interest.

"Oh, they must have reached the road by this time," and Neale went on again. "I guess we needn't bother about them."

But after a moment he said, in a puzzled tone: "That fellow dodged behind the shed as though he did not want to be seen. Funny——"

"They might steal some of our things," Agnes said. "We ought not to leave the place unguarded. Come on back, Neale."

"Well—maybe you are right," admitted the boy. "Though probably they are harmless folks."

"They could steal the automobiles," declared Agnes.

"Now, don't work yourself up into a conniption fit," chuckled Neale. "You think everybody you see is an automobile thief."

"Oh! what's that?"

The sudden sputtering of an engine was audible. Somebody was trying the starter of the runabout they had left standing in the shade before the barn.

"Fooling with it, of course!" muttered Neale, starting to run.

"They are stealing it!" whispered Agnes, determined to believe the worst.

It seemed as though, on this occasion, Agnes was right. As they dashed around the corner of the stable and reached the open yard, the runabout began to "chug-chug" regularly, and they saw it being steered out of the Higgins premises.

"Hey, there! Stop!" yelled Neale.

"Oh, Neale!" wailed Agnes. "It's that Saleratus Joe and the ugly man."

She was correct. The freckled-faced fellow who had been Mr. Jim Brady's chauffeur was driving the re-stolen automobile, while the ugly man sat beside him. The latter turned around and laughed at the excited boy and girl as the runabout swerved into the road and took the direction of the railroad at a fast clip.

"Oh, dear me! what will Mrs. Heard say?" gasped Agnes.

"What will Mr. Collinger say? That's more to the point," growled Neale. "Who would have thought that those fellows were around here? And there's the can they brought with them. Gasoline, of course. They didn't have to use it, for the tank of the runabout is nearly full."

"What shall we do, Neale?" cried Agnes.

Neale was practical, when once he recovered from his first amazement. He dashed into the barn and swung open the big doors.

"They didn't see our car," he cried. "And let me tell you they can't get away from it. I can drive our car much faster than they can run that little one—believe me!"

He tried the starter, glanced into the gas tank, and then got in behind the steering wheel.

"Well, Neale O'Neil!" cried Agnes. "You're not going alone—not much!"

As the car started she swung herself aboard. Neale said, hastily:

"I don't know about your going with me, Aggie. There may be trouble——"

"I don't care. I'm going," she said, with determination. "I wouldn't miss this for a farm!"

"Hang on!" he cried, as the big car rumbled out of the barn.

The mechanism worked all right, and when they turned into the road the stolen motor car was not yet out of sight.

"And we won't let it get out of sight," Neale declared. "I just wish we'd run into that Sheriff Keech again. But he lives a long way from here."

"Why, Neale!" laughed his girl companion, "he isn't even sheriff over here. Don't you remember that we're in another county now?"

"Cracky! I'd forgotten that. Well, we've got no pull with the officers of the law in this county, perhaps; but neither has Saleratus Joe. I'm going to hang right to those fellows until there's a chance of getting them arrested."

For once Agnes was satisfied with the speed of the car. It roared along the road, jolting over the uneven spots, thundering over a wooden bridge which spanned a creek, finally shooting into the main highway to the railroad station, not a hundred yards behind the stolen car.

By this time the ugly man, who often looked around, was not laughing at the Corner House girl and her companion. Without doubt Saleratus Joe was driving the runabout at top speed; but the small car did not have the powerful engine that had been built into the larger car.

They passed nobody on the road—no vehicle at least. And that was a good thing, too; for almost any horse would have been frightened by the onrush of the two cars.

"What do you suppose they mean to do? Where are they going?" shouted Agnes in Neale's ear.

"I haven't the least idea," returned the boy. "But I know what I'm going to do."

"What is that?" she asked.

"Hang to 'em! Hang just like a bulldog to a tramp's coat-tail," declared Neale O'Neil.

At that moment the little station at Hickton came into sight. There were two men, talking excitedly, standing directly in the middle of the highway, and, when they sighted these two men, the thieves in the runabout slowed down.

CHAPTER XXV—WELCOME HOME

"Oh, Neale!" gasped Agnes, hanging to his arm as the big car came roaring down to the Hickton railway station. "Oh, Neale! that's that horrid Brady man."

It was plain to be seen that one of the men in the middle of the road was the Milton politician, Jim Brady. But the other man——

"It's the surveyor. I know him," whispered Neale, shutting off the engine. "Mr. Philip Collinger, Mrs. Heard's nephew. It's all over now but the shouting, Aggie. I bet he doesn't let that car of his get away again."

Indeed, the two men from Milton had stopped the runabout, and the freckled-faced fellow and the ugly man with him were caught, red-handed.

"Get out of my car!" Neale and Agnes heard Mr. Collinger command the two rascals. "I'd like to know how you got it again? I know that it was in the hands of friends of mine yesterday. This henchman of yours, Brady, is a born thief."

"He's a born fool," growled the fat man, mopping his bald brow and glaring at the cringing Joe.

The other fellow was quietly slipping around the corner of the railroad station. He was not going to be present during this altercation.

"He's something besides a fool," said Mr. Collinger sternly. "It's you, Brady, who have shown a lack of wit. I know very well you put this fellow up to taking my car because you thought I was carrying those road maps around in it."

"You think a whole lot, Collinger," snarled the big man. "But you can't prove a thing."

"No. Not unless Joe, here, turns state's evidence, and he wouldn't dare do that. I know the sort of hold you have on such fellows, Brady. But, nevertheless, you are the goat in this matter."

"Huh?" queried the politician.

Mr. Collinger went to his car, drawing a bunch of keys from his pocket as he did so. He selected a flat key and quickly inserted it in a tiny aperture in the face-panel of the seat—an aperture that the uninitiated would never dream was a keyhole.

To the amazement of all, the county surveyor slipped aside the panel and displayed a shallow closet filled with rolls of parchment.

"Just what I thought, Brady," he said, with scorn. "You had 'em in the stolen auto all the time. Now the time has come to deliver them to the commission and I sha'n't carry them any more. Now, who was the fool, Brady?"

But the big man was stamping away to the platform. Saleratus Joe slunk after him like a whipped cur.

"You are two of the young folks my aunt is traveling with, I take it?" said Mr. Collinger, turning to Neale and Agnes. "And I guess you were chasing those fellows."

"Yes, Mr. Collinger," Agnes said. "And they would not have got away from us."

"I am sure they would not," he returned, smiling. "Tell me about it."

So the story was told, and then Mr. Collinger decided to drive back to the Higgins place and see Mrs. Heard before starting for Milton. He was warm in his praise of the Corner House girls and Neale, as well as of Sammy Pinkney, for what they had done toward aiding him in securing the car.

The girls did not understand fully the reasons underlying the stealing of the runabout, or why Mr. Collinger did not intend to prosecute Jim Brady and the freckled-faced man.

"I wouldn't make anything out of it," the surveyor said. "And I have the car back and, best of all, the maps and papers they wanted to get from me. I am satisfied."

He remained to dinner with the touring party, and then started back for Milton. But it was not the intention of the Corner House girls and their party to go home immediately.

They spent four more days on the road—days of pure delight for all the Kenway sisters, for even Sammy behaved well during that part of the tour.

Yet, after all, they were glad to get home when the car rolled up to the Willow Street gate of the Stower homestead. Mrs. MacCall and Linda ran out of the gate to welcome them. Uncle Rufus hobbled around from the garden, swinging his tattered straw hat and cheering. Even Aunt Sarah Maltby appeared on the porch to welcome somewhat grimly her nieces and Neale O'Neil.

Then, from across the street came Mrs. Pinkney, with a delighted scream of welcome.

"Oh, Sammy! How you've grown!" she declared, when she had hugged and kissed the would-be pirate, and then stood off to look at him.

"Huh! that's Ruth's fault," he said. "She made me wash so often. You know, watering things like that is what makes 'em grow."

"This Corner House is the loneliest place in the world without you lassies in it," declared Mrs. MacCall, having hugged the four girls in rotation, and then started all over again.

Aunt Sarah expressed herself as glad to see her nieces again. "As long as you haven't been killed in that automobile, I presume we should all be thankful," she said. "But I did not expect to see you all return with whole bones."

"And one time, when me and Tess were lost, and before we found the Gypsies," confessed Dot, "I thought that funny bone in my back was broke, Aunt Sarah. But it got mended again."

There was a regular "party" of all the Corner House girls' young friends soon after their return, and the adventures of the tour by automobile were related to everybody.

Ruth could remember all about the beautiful scenery they saw and the queer old inns they stopped at. She really had gained much entertainment from the trip.

Agnes' mind was full of the incidents of the stolen automobile, and how it had been found, and how she and Neale had chased the thieves to the Hickton station where the car was captured. To hear her tell it, it had been a most exciting time.

Dot's mind seemed full of the Gypsies and her adventures with Tess when they were lost and had slept all night under a tree. "And that old owl that shouted at us and wanted to know our names," she said. "Just as plain as could be, he hollered: 'Who? Who? Who?'"

But Tess was thoughtful. Somebody asked her what she was thinking of.

"Why, I'll tell you," said the next to the smallest Corner House girl. "I can't get over Neale being so—so stingy. I've asked him, and I've asked him, and he just won't."

"He won't what?"

"Why, he won't tell me what he whispered into the ear of Mrs. Heard's brown pony to make him go. And I think he might!"

THE END

Milton Keynes UK
Ingram Content Group UK Ltd.
UKHW022003250624
444714UK00010B/424